T0034673

A SEASON OF MONSTROUS CONCEPTIONS

A SEASON OF MONSTROUS CONCEPTIONS

LINA RATHER

TOR PUBLISHING GROUP
New York

A SEASON OF MONSTROUS CONCEPTIONS

A Tordotcom Book
Published by Tom Doherty Associates / Tor Publishing Group
120 Broadway
New York, NY 10271

www.tor.com

Tor® is a registered trademark of Macmillan Publishing Group, LLC.

The Library of Congress Cataloging-in-Publication Data
is available upon request.

ISBN 978-1-250-88401-5 (hardcover)
ISBN 978-1-250-87123-7 (ebook)

Our books may be purchased in bulk for promotional, educational, or business use. Please contact your local bookseller or the Macmillan Corporate and Premium Sales Department at 1-800-221-7945, extension 5442, or by email at MacmillanSpecialMarkets@macmillan.com.

First Edition: 2023

Printed in the United States of America

0 9 8 7 6 5 4 3 2 1

A SEASON OF MONSTROUS CONCEPTIONS

CHAPTER 1

LONDON

January 1675

A cold year in a spate of them

Sarah knew Rebecca's babe was dead as soon as the head slid free, from the look on Mistress June's face. She was not so long into her midwifery apprenticeship, but she'd learned what that look meant early. And by the time the first arm was out, it was obvious—this was not a baby meant to survive in this world. It had gills on its neck and a neat line of scales down its back like the hooks up the spine of a good woman's stay. It would have been a problem anyway, had it lived. There was nothing to be done for these ones, no way to hide them.

Outside, the night wind howled and shook the shutters, trying to claw its way into the room they'd finally managed to make warm. Steam rose off the pile of rags on the floor, all of them used to sop up the blood and vomit and slick fluids of the past hours. She knew that some of the blood had surely made it between the floorboards and was likely dripping down into the printshop below, where the husband waited for someone to tell him the child had come into the world. The thumping of the press reverberated up through the ceiling beams and Sarah's knees as she knelt on the floor. The air was tangy on her tongue. Here on Fleet Street, everything stank of iron ink and sweat. The ink and the blood together made the air taste like she was licking a farthing coin, and despite her training, acid rose in the back of her throat.

"Sarah," Mrs. June said. "Get me some clean cloths." She slid two fingers behind the baby's back. One arm free, but the other shoulder was caught. Rebecca hissed when Mrs. June pressed inside her, but she had no strength anymore for wailing. *We had some trouble with her others,* Mrs. June had said, before they arrived. *Very narrow pelvis; be prepared.*

Sarah did as she was bid. By the time she returned from the front room, where the pot of water boiled over the fire and the mother's mother and aunts waited, Mrs. June had the rest of it birthed.

"He hasn't cried." Rebecca had three babes before this one. She panted, but her eyes were glassy with pain and exhaustion. The other three were girls, and it was well known that her husband wished a boy for an apprentice.

Mrs. June took the cloths from Sarah, clipped the baby's cord with a sharp knife she kept for the purpose, and wrapped it up with a practiced hand so all but its face was hidden. The mother tried to rise from the birthing chair, but she still had one leg propped on Mrs. June's shoulder and she was too tired after nine hours of laboring to coordinate herself.

"It's as I feared." Mrs. June patted Rebecca's knee. Rebecca turned her face against the high back of the chair. "Would you like to hold him?"

"Show me his face."

Mrs. June passed the swaddled bundle to Sarah and stayed on the floor, where she could watch the afterbirth. It all had to come in one piece, else the mother was more likely to contract childbed fever. In the six months of her apprenticeship, Sarah had thus far seen two women die of the fever. She didn't wish to see a third, so she took the babe, though she also didn't wish to look upon it. She held out the baby and Rebecca pressed a finger against his little lips. Like pansy buds.

"His face ain't right," Rebecca said.

It wasn't. He had very large eyes, like a creature meant for the dark.

Mrs. June looked at Sarah, silent. Sarah swallowed. In the beginning of her training, she'd been trusted only to boil the pot and bring cloths. Now she'd progressed to checking the mother's progress into labor and, apparently, explaining when something went wrong. Though there was no explaining a thing like this. You put a thing like this in the Lord's hands and well, He was unlikely to explain

Himself, wasn't he? Sometimes she thought the papists had the right of it, with all their burying saints' icons and lighting candles. Witchcraft, the bishops called it, but if it helped a child quicken right in the womb, then it seemed helpful enough. Though she knew the papists of London were birthing the same kinds of babies the Protestants were these days. Babies like this creature born to breathe in dark waters.

"This happens sometimes. It ain't made right inside you, that's all."

Rebecca hiccuped, and a tear rolled down her plump cheek to her chin where it mixed with the sweat that still glistened there from her exertion.

"Come now," Mrs. June said. "There will be more babies after this one. It's just the way of the world. You and William are young yet, and there will be sons aplenty." Rebecca's hand loosened around the bundle and Mrs. June took it back from her, gently. "We'll take it to the church for you, and you'll think on it no more. I shall get your mother, and once the afterbirth is passed you can have your rest." She slipped so easily from *he* to *it*. Sarah saw Rebecca start to slip that way, too. Easier not to think about it. Easier to give them the extra money for a stillbirth's burial in the churchyard and put this matter from her mind, except perhaps for when she went to services, and crossed the ground where he would be buried, and thought about which bit of grass might hide her dead child.

4

Rebecca descended into silence. The sun fell, too, while Mrs. June and Sarah waited for the last of the afterbirth to deliver itself. It was an easy enough labor, all told, aside from the baby's body cooling on the bedside table. Finally, it was as over as it could be and Mrs. June let the grandmother into the room to see to Rebecca. Her face was still and soft and she wiped the sweat off Rebecca's brow with the hem of her apron, like Rebecca was a barefoot child again and not a woman who had just delivered a child of her own. While they were distracted, Mrs. June opened her bag and tucked the baby inside on top of her books and medicines, snug up like it was in danger of catching another death.

Sarah helped Rebecca clean herself. It had been a longer labor than her last, and with the blood and fluid dried, Sarah could see that her flesh had torn. She looked up toward Mrs. June, who examined the bleeding gash and then laid her hand on Rebecca's stomach once more. Her lips moved almost imperceptibly and Sarah felt the air shudder. She shivered, but Rebecca and her mother noticed nothing at all, of course. When Mrs. June finished, the flesh had healed itself with only the smallest of silver scars, as thin as spider silk, to remember the trauma.

"Fresh underskirts for the next several weeks," Mrs. June said, as much to the grandmother as to Rebecca. "Teach the little ones to do the wash if you can't manage."

Sarah stood. Her knees ached from kneeling on the

plank floor. The sounds from the printshop on the house's ground floor had faded with the sun, and now she heard Rebecca's husband in the next room bringing something to a boil over the kitchen fire. One of the girls whined about the chill, whined and whined until there came the sharp smack of a hand against a small face and she cut off in a little sob. Then Sarah heard the husband gasp and the sound of the lid of the stewpot being thrown back down. So the grandmother had told him he wouldn't be getting a son today. She supposed there was nothing else for him to do but rage at it. Some men, when they heard that their baby had been born still and wouldn't even have the dignity of being buried in the consecrated section of the churchyard, preferred to simply pretend that there had never been a baby at all. Some of them decided to turn their rage on their wives, for there were many men who believed that for a pregnancy to end in a stillbirth meant their wife had wished it. Better for him to rage at the rest of the world and be finished with it.

"It's my fault," Rebecca mumbled, with her cheek pressed against the back of the chair. "I brought this upon my baby."

"Of course not," Sarah said, and patted her gently on the arm, and moved to finish packing up their instruments. But Rebecca gripped her hard around the wrist. Hard enough that Sarah yelped, and Mrs. June stopped her own packing to look up. Rebecca's hand was hot as the inside of a baker's brick oven and slick with sweat. She hadn't been fevered before, and should not be fevered now either—no fever came on this fast. This was just her burning herself up from the inside with sadness.

"I looked upon it," Rebecca said. Her mother mumbled something soft and soothing but she might as well have not spoken at all. Rebecca's fingernails dug into Sarah's wrist and she was sure there would be blood in a moment. "Late at night, before the baby had quickened. I was out on the street and I looked upon the Devil himself, or one of his creatures—fur and horn and bone, nothing that should have walked this earth. And I know, I know it stamped itself onto my baby and made it not right. I know my letters. I read Culpeper's book. I know that's how it happens when the baby's made wrong."

"Now, now." Mrs. June pried Rebecca's hand off of Sarah. "There's much wickeder places in the world than London, and that's where the Devil's spending his time. It was only a bad dream."

"I saw it," Rebecca said. But her head slipped to lean against her mother's stomach. "I saw it and it pressed itself into my mind, and it made my baby a monster." Her mother stroked her hair, and her eyes closed, though Sarah saw tears welling beneath them still.

"Call upon us if anything changes," Mrs. June said.

Rebecca's mother shook her head. "I told her to stay in bed myself. Too much work to be done in the shop, she said. Well, look now. We live next to a fisherman who took his wife out on the boat when she was far too late along. Got scared half to death by some fish and their baby came out with webbing between its fingers. Suppose that can't kill you, but what kind of woman will take a husband like that, eh? But there's more of them than there used to be. Seems every week at services they're baptizing a baby who has to be kept covered up."

Mrs. June pressed her lips together. "Even the Greeks spoke of children with webbed fingers. Only natural variation." But the grandmother shook her head, as if to say, *But there's much more than that afoot, isn't there?* And there was, for Sarah had delivered two other babies like Rebecca's this winter already. One had also been too uncanny to survive; the other had lived, but by the way its father looked upon its feathered feet, Sarah feared for it. In the pubs and the markets, people whispered about strange shadows seen at dusk, misshapen bodies glimpsed just around the next corner or at the end of alleys too distant for the weak light of the streetlamps to reach. Some of the more superstitious took fervently to their pews and spoke about the end of all days. The crueler kind turned their fear on beggars with clubbed feet or missing limbs, as if these common afflictions were tied to the stranger ones being birthed by the dozens. Sarah had not heard of a terror like this in the city outside of stories of the Great Fire, when all of London stood together in the ashes and broken stone, on streets that had so recently run with the molten lead from burning churches. Less than a decade on and here was the city coming apart again, even as Sir Christopher Wren's monument to the fire rose brick by brick at one end of London Bridge and promised that the city would not burn again.

Mrs. June considered her next words carefully, treading the line between comfort and lies. "Both Aristotle and Mr. Culpeper were very intelligent men, but even their great abundance of learning cannot explain every twist of creation."

The grandmother cupped the back of Rebecca's head, with her palm covering her daughter's ear, like that might stop her hearing. "And some things are beyond nature. Go on, then. William will have your fee. Take that thing away with you so we can stop speaking of it in this house."

Sarah felt Mrs. June reach into the universe with the last bit of her power.

"Of course," Mrs. June said, and there was a certain resonance to the words that they should not have carried. It took the anger from the grandmother's eyes, and she merely shook her head at them. Sarah lifted the bag with the baby's body swaddled inside—barely heavier than before—and held it against her skirts to hide it from Rebecca's view. They descended the stairs in a hush, past the husband sitting still and silent at his desk and his workers lingering awkwardly about their presses and ink.

Outside, the night air was finally tamping down the

LINA RATHER

daily stink of the manure and waste that ran the gutters. Men lingered in the light bleeding from the window of a pub, drinking the house brew. Mrs. June stopped at the end of the street and gestured to Sarah for the bag.

She undid the clasp and pulled back the rags to reveal the little one's face. Its scales and translucent skin glistened. Mrs. June turned its head to the side with a finger, exposing the dark slashes on its neck.

"Pity," she said. "Perhaps it'd have lived if we threw it in the river in time." With that, she snapped the bag closed again and they continued home in the falling dark.

CHAPTER 2

The next morning, Mrs. June took the dead whelp's body to the parish priest by herself and sent Sarah with a list to the butcher's.

Sarah had accompanied Mrs. June bringing a baby to be buried only once. The priest had looked upon her and sighed the way one might sigh at a fishmonger trying to sell a trout that had gone off, and said, *Found one of your pets, Meredith?* Mrs. June had never brought her again. It turned her stomach that he had seen her and known she was not entirely of this world. She had no mark upon her, not anymore, not like the babies being born this season. She hated that no one would tell her what still marked her as strange.

When her mother was in a mood or too deep in her drink, she often reminded Sarah that she, too, should have been a dead baby buried deep in unconsecrated ground. A generation ago, she'd have been drowned in the river without a thought. And with five siblings before her, there had already been too many mouths to feed and too many more surely coming. The midwife attending would have turned a blind eye and sworn to the court that she was stillborn, or so her mother liked to say. When Sarah touched the scar, she could still feel a nubbin of bone beneath the skin, where her grandmother had snipped the white-furred tail clean off with her sewing scissors before the midwife could see.

Sarah never would have known what the tail really meant, how very strange she really was, had Mrs. June not spotted it in her and offered her an apprenticeship.

She didn't mind a midwife's work—it might not've been what she'd have picked had she had all the options in the world like men did, but it was more satisfaction than beating the same herd of sheep up and down a damp hill year after year—and she'd have her own license by twenty-three. Back in Cookham, she'd likely be married again with a baby of her own, had the crops been bad for another year running and her parents unable to maintain her in their household through a hungry winter. Or she might have met a bloodier end, had the whispers in the village grown until the magistrate tried her for the murder they all suspected her of, or she would have had to flee to London anyway for a far less respectable occupation.

This was why she did not believe she was a demon, like so many in London whispered the strange children were. In her darkest hour, newly widowed and about to be run out of the village or strung up or worse, Mrs. June had appeared and offered her a new life. And what could that be, save Providence?

But she did not like to think about what had happened in Cookham. This morning, it weighed too heavily on her, and she tried to shake the dark thoughts free as she stepped past a half-frozen puddle in the street.

A fancy caught her, and she stopped over the puddle. More mud than water, truly, but enough to reflect the angles of her face. She leaned over it, and thought she might see this time what marked her out—some strange glow perhaps—

From across the lane, a woman yelped in pain. A rag-collector's mule startled and stamped in the puddle, splattering Sarah top to bottom in muck. She leapt back but the driver took no notice. Some manners. Lucky she hadn't already purchased the roast Mrs. June had sent her for. Quite a messy task, rinsing flecks of street grime off a good piece of meat, and there would always be a bit of grit left in. She looked across the street to where the cry had come from, and saw a woman clearly with child doubled over against the front of a bakery, one hand clutching the sill, the other supporting her belly.

The roast would wait.

The woman was clearly wealthy. A string of pearls looped around her neck to match the drops in her ears, and her dress was cut with the newly fashionable square neckline that exposed the slope of her collarbones and the tops of her pale shoulders. One of Mrs. June's rules of business was *Always take lodgings on the most prestigious street you can afford, as most of your customers will come from close by.* But while this was a good neighborhood—full of the sort of men who sold things that other people made, rather than selling the labor of their own two hands, and the kind of women who sewed new aprons for their hired midwives—it was not the sort where the women wore pearls every day. A woman like this likely had already retained a midwife. May have paid extra to retain her woman exclusively for her lying-in period, even. But as Mrs. June said, there was no harm in advertising one's services regularly and well.

"I'm a midwife," Sarah said. "Can I help?"

The woman huffed out another pained breath. She gave Sarah a look full of doubt. Sarah didn't look quite old enough to have birthed many children of her own, which was how a woman usually gauged a midwife's experience. And indeed, she had no children—only the fact of her widowhood lent her the respectability necessary for her profession. And even then, she and Mrs. June had obfuscated the true length and depth of her marriage. Plenty of their clients asked her polite questions that clearly assumed her children were living with a sister or brother of hers better able to provide for them.

"An apprentice," Sarah amended, and the woman gestured her closer.

"It just sprung upon me," she said, and rubbed her gravid

stomach right under where her navel would be. "Here. A strong pain, almost like—*oof.*"

"Is this your first?" Sarah asked, though she guessed her new patient was thirty at least and not a naive new wife. The woman did not look far enough gone for labor, but it was often hard to tell.

"My second." Something flickered across the woman's face, that pain particular to the mothers of stillbirths and children cut down while still in bonnets. Well. Since this was not her first, she likely was not simply surprised by the normal discomforts of pregnancy. Some young girls came wailing to Mrs. June when they were barely five months along with their firsts, moaning about how their feet hurt and their backs pained them, and might this be it already?

Sarah pressed her hand against the woman's stomach. The baby pressed back against her hand. She was carrying low—a boy, if Sarah had to wager. "Bend your hips a bit. Stretch out slowly."

The woman did so, and when the pain lessened, she sighed in relief.

"There is a ligament that tends to tighten in this stage," Sarah explained. "Especially if you move too quickly. Simple stretching will sort you out." The woman took a deep breath in and out and grimaced again, but the worst of it had passed; she straightened up and fixed her fine clothing back into neatness. Sarah eyed her fashion again. Women dressed like this usually had maids to do their shopping for them and spent their days doing needlework or visiting friends. Perhaps she was newly without means. It would not be the first time that a husband had gambled away all a couple's money or poured it into a business venture that sank to the bottom of the ocean. Families were ruined by the whims of the sea every day. "Are you new to London, Mrs.—"

"Lady Faith." If she took offense at Sarah's mistaking her title, she didn't show it, but it threw her fine attire into a new light. Lady Faith smoothed her apron and now Sarah saw she was clutching a shopping list in her other hand. A woman raised with her letters then, born into a good family as well as married into one. "Faith Wren. And you are Miss—"

"Mrs. Sarah Davis. My husband"—now Sarah's breath hitched, and she made herself smile through it, hid it behind a broadside seller shouting his wares behind them— "has left us, unfortunately."

"My condolences," Faith Wren said, politely.

"It was some time ago." She probably should have added more, spoken of a cherished memory or what a good man he had been. But all her memories of him were also of hunger and hard work, and while she could not call him cruel, she also could not call him loving or kind. She had been for him just a new acquisition, an expected step in his life, convenient to provide him with food and mended clothing and children. And he had been for her just a way to greater security, for when she was barely fourteen, her parents had made it clear they could no longer sustain her in their house, and her skills in cooking and domestic work were far from exceptional enough to find work in a fine household, but good enough for a husband.

Faith seemed content with her answer. "My husband is working nearby, so for now we are keeping our home in London. My family, though, is in Oxfordshire." She smiled slightly. "Perhaps you could tell me, with your experience—do you think I will be having a daughter? Or a son?"

"Which do you wish for?" Sarah asked. She could say she guessed a boy, but she saw here a woman who wanted conversation more than she wanted a midwife's skills. This was what she liked best about the profession. She liked people, and being a midwife gave her access to all kinds. She had delivered babies for fishmongers' wives and women whose husbands traded with the Orient, who reclined on sofas upholstered in silk while they heaved new life into the world. Once, she'd even attended a baroness's daughter when her chosen midwife had been taken by a fever only two days before the delivery and Mrs. June had been called instead.

"My first child was a son. My husband wishes for another, so that he can pass on his learning."

"Husbands often wish for sons. May I?" Sarah pressed her hand underneath the heft of Faith's stomach again and palpated the womb. She was further along than Sarah had first anticipated, based on how the babe lay firmly against the abdominal wall. As much as Mrs. June despised the doctors for their torturous devices and derision toward midwives' hand-down wisdom, she still bought their anatomy texts and showed Sarah the way a woman's body changed when she carried a baby this late. The hips turned, the pubic bone split and opened, the stomach muscles that crossed an empty womb tore to accommodate new fullness. This babe was no more than seven months along, but already it was out of room; Sarah felt the bend of its elbow pressed against Faith's taut flesh. Nearly all the water in the womb was gone.

She found its head, turning as it should toward the pelvis, and that was when she felt it, like a bolt of lightning that leapt up her arm and down her spine and froze her in place in shock and awe. It was as if a door had opened in front of her, a door into one of the grand cathedrals built in ages past that stunned you with its divine scale, and now she could do nothing but gape at it.

"Sometimes I wish for a daughter for a companion." Faith, oblivious to the strangeness that had overtaken Sarah, pointed to the narrow line of the Monument to the Great Fire of London rising over the houses some streets away. "My husband is an accomplished man—that is his work, there—but he keeps eccentric company and few of them have wives for me to find companionship with. Though in the end, having lost Gilbert so terribly, I suppose I only want this child to live."

Sarah could not say, *This child will live,* even though she knew it as firmly as she knew there was solid ground under her feet and the sky would not fall from the heavens onto her head. She felt the child's heart beating with a dark and terrible power. She felt it like a key fitting into a lock, that heavy iron clunk of gears turning. Her mouth had gone dry. Strange visions tumbled through her mind, of landscapes twisting upon themselves and a fractured storm-racked sky, and she could not say if it was a dark imagining or a window opened from this street to a terrible, sideways world.

Faith moved, and when the baby's head was gone from under her hand, the spell broke. Sarah's legs trembled.

"The first one was easy as anything," Faith said. Now that she'd started talking, it seemed there was nothing to stop her. Their differences in position did not seem to matter in the slightest. Nor did she seem to notice the sweat that Sarah felt trickling down her hairline. She must look like she'd just broken the grip of a fever. Or she felt as if she did, at least. "Never had a pain at all with Gilbert, not until the labor started. He came so fast that the midwife did not make it to the doorstep. She was very disappointing, in any case. I think her lateness was better explained by her habit for drink than by my quick laboring. Are you currently reserved, Mrs. Davis?"

"I am only an apprentice," Sarah reminded her.

Faith waved a hand. It was the sort of gesture that the titled class used when they were confident that someone else would work out any inconvenient details. "Come with me. I shall introduce you to my husband. He has his own ideas, but is often susceptible to my persuasion."

Sarah followed along behind, and it wasn't until the next street over that it struck her that Lady Faith had pointed at the Monument and called it her husband's work. Could it be? Sarah had read about the famed Sir Christopher Wren in the papers, same as any Londoner with their letters. He was one of the brightest stars of the new generation of virtuosos, they said, as accomplished at medicine and physics as he was in architecture. They said he'd created marvelous inventions when only a child. When he had been appointed Surveyor of the King's Works five years ago, the news had even made it all the way to her sheep-stinking village of Cookham. Forget her protestations that she wasn't licensed herself yet, and forget the roast she'd been sent out for— she couldn't imagine the pride on Mrs. June's face if she returned with a commission like this instead.

Faith hurried on despite her condition, and they made it to the Monument before the watery January sun had crossed much farther across the sky. Despite the chilling damp that numbed Sarah's toes, the streets bustled with house staff, all grumbling as they did the errands for masters and mistresses snug up at home. Sarah had seen the construction rising, of course, but she had not yet come to gawk herself. The white stone edifice would be topped with a golden flame, and two workmen balanced up there on spindly scaffolding now, finishing the understructure. Another man in rolled shirtsleeves lounged against the base of the monument, consulting something on a long sheet of vellum. When he saw them approaching, he smiled, lay the plans aside on a worktable, and came to meet them. He placed his hand on Faith's elbow and kissed her lightly on the cheek. "Hello, my dear."

She sighed at him in mock rebuke, and produced a lump wrapped in a tea towel from her apron pocket. "You forgot."

Sir Christopher Wren unwrapped the towel to reveal a hand pie, and sank his teeth into it with undignified gusto. A bit of browned meat—lamb, from the smell—escaped the pastry and landed on his collar.

"This is Mrs. Davis," Faith said, and brought Sarah forward with a small tug on her sleeve. "She is a midwife, and she lent me some assistance earlier."

"Assistance." Wren's eyes went to her stomach and the pie for a moment hung forgotten halfway to his mouth. Childbirth was the domain of women, and it would be impolite for him to ask the questions he so clearly wanted to, especially in front of a stranger. Sarah found the concern touching, even unvoiced. So many men forgot their seed was half the child and lay all the responsibility for it at the feet of their wives, especially if something went wrong. His worry did not have that angry edge to it.

"Normal pains," Sarah said, and tried her best to hide her village accent. "The baby's getting ready is all."

"I would like to hire her," Faith said. At this, Wren sighed and dug into the pie again. "For all your learning, Christopher, this is one area where you are hardly the expert. Your inclination is at best highly unusual." She turned to Sarah and leaned in conspiratorially. "He was planning on delivering it himself."

Shocking. Sarah couldn't help but lean away from the man, like his lunacy might be catching. Allowing a man in the birthing room was bad enough—but allowing him to oversee it! Unusual—no, it was unnatural.

"For the good of the knowledge of mankind," Wren said. "Really, Faith, you make it sound like a passing fancy. Yes, Mrs. Davis, it would be unusual, but anatomists rarely get to dissect a pregnant woman, and so the mechanics of procreation are still a great mystery. We do not properly understand how a child comes to be, why some are born alive and some dead, some sickly and others hale. We don't know what determines the sex of a child. Look what's in the papers these days—children with fangs like dogs and fur like river otters, and they say there is some terrible countenance stalking the streets that imprints itself onto the mothers' wombs. What mechanism controls such malformations? I cannot produce a gravid body to dissect, but

I can observe the end of the process, which may provide some illumination. And male midwives are not as uncommon as they once were. Why, I just read an account in the *Lancet* from a surgeon who saved a breech baby using a mechanical device of his own creation."

Sarah glanced sidelong at Faith. She looked rather less disturbed by this speech than Sarah thought she ought to.

"Mrs. Davis is a professional," she said as if Sir Christopher's lack of experience in the art of midwifery was the only objectionable thing here.

"And while there may be some men who have taken up midwifery," Sarah added hastily, "to have a man in the birthing room, and one's own husband no less—" She remembered too late who it was that she was speaking to and tried to find words other than *improper* or *a shame*. Incapable of holding her tongue, Mrs. June liked to say. It had gotten her in trouble more than once. She closed her mouth and felt the commission slipping through her fingers.

"You see, you're scandalizing her." Faith took her elbow like they were old friends. This whole conversation had the cadence of a well-worn joke, one that Sarah wasn't in on. All she knew was she had to deliver this baby. For what she had felt in it. Whatever it was, she knew it would not come looking merely human, and she could not imagine what a man so fascinated with the workings of the body might think of his own monstrous child, or use it for.

"All for the benefit of mankind," Wren repeated, though

because he said it somewhat petulantly and with most of a pastry crust in his mouth, it did not have the gravity such a pronouncement should.

"He shall be in the room," Faith said, this time to Sarah. "It is unusual, but I have an unusual husband. Will you still accept?"

Sarah looked at Wren. The great genius still had a speck of lamb clinging to his collar. He was a slight man, and wore a countenance that said he was not used to being turned down. Sarah considered Mrs. June's usual fee, added a hefty surcharge both for the matter of the husband and the quality of Faith's pearls, and named it. Both of the Wrens nodded, together.

"Very well," Wren said. He already seemed to be losing interest and picked the architectural plans back up from the worktable. He frowned at them, then at the two men up at the top of the column. "If that is what you will allow, dear, I suppose I will make do."

Sarah and Faith worked out the details easily enough; this interested Wren not at all. The women bade each other farewell and Faith left just ahead of Sarah, her attention already on another errand, leaving Sir Christopher once more absorbed in his work. Sarah had thought she had vanished entirely from his mind until she stepped off the curb into the bustling roadway.

"Mrs. Davis, a question," he said. "Have you delivered any of those unusual children?"

Unusual was a funny way of phrasing it. All of the gossip she heard on the streets used much stronger language. "Yes. Hard to find a London midwife that hasn't, now."

She thought he might ask more questions—braced herself to become part of the business of *scientific inquiry*— but he merely nodded and dismissed her with a wave of his hand.

CHAPTER 3

Explaining the matter of the Wren baby proved more straightforward than Sarah had expected. When she returned to the rooms she shared with Mrs. June—her errand to the butcher completely forgotten—and laid out the story of her new acquaintance, her mistress soaked it in with that gleam in her eye that said she was already counting the shillings.

"This is excellent," she said. "Far along, you say? And you already arranged an appointment for us? Wonderful. Her husband has such fashionable pursuits. In the papers all the time. We could get so many referrals! You may have set yourself up, Sarah. Once you have your own license—or enough good word behind you that you don't need the formality—here's your client base."

"Her baby." Sarah hadn't gotten to this part yet. "When I felt for it . . ."

Mrs. June paused midway through measuring out her various tinctures and powders for her bag. Some were medicine, some witchcraft, and some were a bit of both. Now she picked up the blade she was using to scrape thyme leaves into the kettle in the hearth. "What was it? Did you feel it, smell it, see it?"

"The baby?"

"Don't be slow, girl. The Other Place." Her knife moved again; small herb leaves fell into the water with a hiss, and the room filled with the comforting green smell of the countryside.

The Other Place, that strange realm where they drew their witchery from. Dangerous to speak of more than was necessary. "Yes. Like a vision of Hell."

"You think it Hell we call on?"

Sarah was thrown. "I don't—I suppose not—" One of the other apprentices thought it Hell, though that seemed silly and simplistic to Sarah.

"I was asking for your opinion." All of Mrs. June's lessons were like this. She gave nothing for free. Every bit of knowledge Sarah got she had to grope her way to in darkness, led only by Mrs. June's disapproval or small pride in equal turn. When she said something wrong, she got a sigh or a slap to the back of the head; when she did something right, it was a small smile or the larger portion of meat on her plate. "Plenty in the streets say the children are demons, or that the Devil came to their mothers in the night and had his way with them. And we both know what that power led you to."

Sarah picked up the next bundle of thyme and plucked the leaves off one by one to have something to do with her hands. Six months, and she had not dared ask questions. This new life was as fragile as a china cup—but the questions ate her up inside.

"Why did you hire me?" If news of her past in Cookham came to London, it would stain them both. She was a dangerous apprentice. "I am sure you had . . . other choices."

"Your kind is actually exceedingly rare." Her kind, the kind touched by the Other Place and marked by it, in blood and bone and strange power. "Well. Not now, I suppose, with all those babies looking like they do. But one like you, old enough to take instruction and to have grown into your powers? A handful in the whole isle, I suspect, perhaps fewer."

Another question occurred to Sarah. "Do you find it strange there are so few men among our number?" One of Mrs. June's friends—a small group of midwives who called themselves a guild, though they had no leave to establish one—had a male apprentice, a sickly boy. He was the only one Sarah knew to have the power, and he did not seem to be marked like she was, unless he hid it beneath his patched clothes.

Mrs. June huffed a laugh. "Hardly. Men get some power, and what do they do? They take to politics and get beheaded, or if they lack the standing for that, they take to prophecy like John Bull, or to spectacular criminality, and find themselves in irons soon enough. Women have enough sense to escape notice." She stirred her pot and thought about it more. "And many men might never discover their gift for it at all. Plenty of other types of power for them.

"Ones like me, we can access a bit of the power of the Other Place, use it to bend the rules of this world in small ways." Mrs. June poured a bit of the tincture into a small cup for Sarah to taste the balance of herbs; another test, though a mundane one. "We can sense a bit of that power, draw it down even as it takes from us in return. But the ones like you—marked by the Other Place, part of it—it runs so much deeper in you. I could never *see* it, you know. That knowledge is only for your kind. I always imagined it was beautiful."

At that last, her voice held a note of wistfulness or disappointment—a pretty fantasy broken.

In Sarah's third week with Mrs. June, Rose Elliot's baby had come with the cord wrapped thrice around its neck, as blue as ice at night, and Sarah had known there was no getting it free quick enough for it to breathe. But Mrs. June had slipped her little finger under it, and then the cord was in two pieces, like she'd cut it. She hadn't—her knife sat clean on the table beside the bed—but the babe was free and bawling. And Mrs. June looked suddenly exhausted, like it hadn't been a quick labor first thing in the morning. Sarah's skin had gone tight and tingling, like she'd been caught in a draft from an open door. Mrs. June had smiled at her, a smile that acknowledged they shared a secret, and just as swiftly Sarah felt that door close again.

Now she turned that memory over and over in her mind, and wondered what she might be able to do after Mrs. June honed her into the blade she wanted.

"What do you think of the tea?" Mrs. June asked.

Sarah scrambled to answer this other test. "More lemon verbena?"

Mrs. June sighed. "This early in the season, the thyme is woody; it has to steep for longer. You must remember these things." She took the cup and filled it again, then set it in front of Sarah with a *thunk*. "And you have plenty still to learn."

Sarah swallowed. She knew what this was; a test she would not pass. Just like she had yet to pass the others. She stared down into the cup. The tea trembled and for a second her heart leapt—but no, it was just her breath rippling the surface. She begged the steam to clear, for the hot tea to turn frigid as she willed it.

"Reach deep," Mrs. June said. Sarah did as she was bid and she could feel the power there, as she always did, like looking through a doorway toward a roaring fire in the next room. But she couldn't touch it any more than she could pull the heat from that fire into a dead hearth. "Come now. You have it. You have so much of it."

And as always, there was a sharp edge of jealousy and

disappointment in Mrs. June's voice. The older woman was one of many—very many—who had a drop of the uncanny blood. Born without a mark, as pretty as any other babe, but with a taste of the power. Like having a window, Mrs. June had said once, where Sarah had a door. And yet Mrs. June could use it at will. Heal a cut or chill a cup of water, unkink a cord or pull a stain from her Sunday clothes. Small witchery, she said, compared to what Sarah might be capable of. If she could ever learn to turn potential into actuality.

All Sarah had ever done was kill a man, a man she had thought she'd loved once, and only when rage had come and taken all her rationality.

"This is very easy," Mrs. June said. She leaned over the table where Sarah sat. "Just chill it. You're not even adding heat, just take it away. Find that lock inside you that opens to somewhere else."

In Sarah's dreams, the Other Place was a nonsense-land, without order or logic, where every misshapen creature or obsidian-black outcropping or flash of purplish lightning crackled with possibility. They were midwives, not naturalists, and the true nature of the Other Place eluded them. One of Mrs. June's fellow midwives said it was another celestial sphere, the way Heaven was a celestial sphere above the earth, this one just much closer to humanity's. This seemed more likely than theories of Hell. Mrs. June had taken her to a lecture on the idea of celestial spheres once. The naturalist had brought out a number of metal rings to show them how the cosmos might fit together—first was the ring representing humanity's sphere of the earth, then another around it to show the stars hovering on another sphere farther above, and finally the third sphere of Heaven, so vast and high above as to be imperceptible from the human vantage. The Other Place could be another ring, set slightly below humanity's, but close enough that it occasionally brushed up against the world and left people like Sarah touched by it.

She closed her eyes and tried to concentrate on those celestial rings. She felt something inside, she thought, a stirring.

The sound of Mrs. June sighing told her she had failed again.

"At least you have decent skills for the babies," Mrs. June said, but Sarah heard exactly what she meant. It was not cheap to feed and house an apprentice, and she had not been chosen for her gentle hands. She could be turned out at any moment, and then what? The entirety of her life rested on her mistress's generosity, just as it had once rested on her husband's, and her parents'.

What must it be to have a life that was not on loan to you? She couldn't think too long about things like that; the despair and want would choke her.

Mrs. June took the cup away and poured the tea back.

No recriminations, no scolding, and somehow that was even worse. "Come along—we'll be late for the guild."

The midwives' guild of the City of London met in the back of a tavern in the shadow of St. Paul's where the proprietor's wife brewed a mediocre ale, but roasted very good hog on her spit and baked decent bread in her oven, and let them rent the back room for a pittance. The guild was not truly a guild, for the crown had not seen fit to grant a group of women a royal charter—not when the doctors and the surgeons all lobbied against it—but that did not stop Mrs. June and the other licensed midwives from muttering about the *Worshipful Company of Midwives* whenever they were a few cups in. It wasn't worth pointing out that their group could not be a guild in any case, as there were only ten of them, hardly a quorum of London's midwives, and they avoided the company of those midwives who only delivered babies as they should. The *Worshipful Company of Witching Midwives* would be accurate, though it would see them all hung.

Sarah sat at a table with the other four apprentices apart from their mistresses. Three of them barely spoke to her. She never knew why, but they looked at her like a chimera in a jar in an apothecary's window. The fourth was the silent boy who was strange not only because of his gender but because he had apparently started as an alchemist's apprentice and been turned out after some unspoken mistake.

Anne spread some pages on the table. Anne was the eleventh of thirteen unlucky children and had taken her apprenticeship to escape an early entry to the nunnery. It had left her with disdain for the Church of England that bordered on blasphemy. "A new surgeon just put out his plates. He favors the theory that a woman is not a man inverted and that the vagina is a separate structure entirely."

Thea pinched up her nose. "Small progress, I suppose. The Greeks believed we were inverted men, and they also believed in humors, and much other ridiculousness besides. They're all dead for a reason. How much is Mistress Constance paying you, anyway, to be buying all these prints?"

Anne blushed. "One of Mr. Johnson's pressmen likes me, I think. He lets me read the pamphlets before the shops get them."

Thea rolled her eyes. Sarah wished she knew either of them well enough to make her own friendly jab, the kind of tease that would bind them together. But they did not look to her. "Forget that—do you know what *I* saw today?" Thea pulled her own page from her apron pocket, swept aside their sherry glasses, and smacked it proudly down.

Another anatomical plate. They'd dissected a baby. Too unseemly for this world. One plate showed its bat wings, one folded and the other stretched out and pinned. Another plate showed its six-eyed face.

Thea read the description to them in a whisper. "This ungodly deformity was birthed from a Yorkshire woman in the Year of Our Lord 1674 and anatomized upon its death. Its blood and bones exhibited promising alchemical traits."

"Promising alchemical traits?" Anne asked.

"Means uncanny."

"We know that." Anne leaned over the drawing. Prurient fascination glowed in her eyes. Sarah tried to examine the drawing—the flaps of skin drawn back with hooks, the feet splayed out—and acid burned the back of her throat. "So many of them now. I saw one of the stillborn ones mummified and stuck up in an apothecarist's window last week. She was claiming a bit of the wing ground into wine would cure a man's impotence or a woman's madness."

"Not like they're in any short supply," Thea muttered. "Mistress Gregory told me before this there might be one of them born a year on the whole isle, if that. Now we're up to one a week in the city, by my count." They both fell silent and looked at Sarah, as if she were the source of this new contagion. She pretended she had not heard and drained her sherry glass. A good bottle today, provided by one of Mrs. Constance's grateful clients. In the opposite corner, Mrs. June and the other full midwives were having a hushed conversation. Mrs. Evans, Thea's mistress, looked up suddenly and beckoned Sarah over.

Sarah imagined she could hear the thoughts of the other apprentices as she rose from the table. *An uncanny girl, a season of uncanny births.* She wondered if they whispered that this were her fault when she wasn't around. They certainly went drinking enough, and though they invited her, she could tell when she was not truly wanted. She refilled her sherry on the way over.

"Sit down," Mrs. Evans said. She was ten years Mrs. June's senior, and in the quiet hierarchy of their false guild, she was at the top. She and Mrs. June were splitting one of the tavern's pork buns; she cut off a corner and pushed it toward Sarah. The oak table was spread with pages that made Sarah's head swim—recipes copied in an old, unfamiliar hand; drawings of strange creatures; geometric images of what seemed to be people standing in formation. "I hear you're very good at your work, my dear. Might've a license of your own before Thea, even." Sarah looked back toward the other apprentices, but they were all pretending not to watch, and were surely too far away to hear.

"Remember when I told you why I chose you?" Mrs. June asked. She picked at her own roast meat, tearing strands of muscle fiber off one by one. The crackling skin squeaked between her teeth.

"We're coming to a time of great power," Mrs. Evans said. She smiled, and not particularly at Sarah. Mrs. Evans's dead husband had been an anatomist, and numerologist, and now Sarah wondered what arcane knowledge from the realm of learned men Mrs. Evans had managed to steal away. "The babies, the way the magic tastes now—you must sense it, with your mark, getting closer."

She did feel it, like someone peering over her shoulder. A looming shadow. Mrs. Evans saw the look on her face and grinned as large as the illuminated demons in a duchess's book of hours. She grabbed Sarah's hand and squeezed until Sarah's bones felt like they'd been turned to mush. "We've seen it coming for years. You don't yet understand what an opportunity this is, but you will. This is a time when the world is soft, and we can shape it, and you will be our tool."

Sarah opened her mouth, but nothing came out. She imagined the world as a ball of clay, smashed flat under her heel, and all the spit dried on her tongue.

"You will do it, of course," Mrs. June said.

"Of course," Sarah whispered. "But . . . how?"

Mrs. Evans let go of her hand and then patted the back of it like a farmer might pet the half-feral cat he keeps in the grain store to scare away the mice. "Very soon, dear. Years of planning has led here—all you will need to do is follow our instructions. We'll all be so proud of you."

Sarah looked at Mrs. June, but her face gave away nothing at all.

CHAPTER 4

When the next stranger appeared at Mrs. June's lodgings in the night, it was not an errand boy of the Wrens, nor any of their other clients in the late stages of pregnancy, but a much grubbier boy who woke her with a stone thrown hard against the window shutter nearest her bed. Sarah slipped from the covers and felt her way to the door, too nervous to curse but wanting to. Mrs. June stirred but did not wake; she had made herself a heavy cup of sack posset that evening.

"What is it?" she whispered to the boy outside, though she suspected.

"One of the ladies of Drury Lane sent for you," he whispered back. He was a small thing, though she guessed around eight. She'd seen him lurking in a corner the last time she had visited that particular house.

She dressed as well as she could in the dark and followed him. She heard the wails before he even unlocked the front door of the house.

Women clustered around the receiving room, some blinking blearily, others clearly fresh from customers and still dressed in their extravagant frills with necklines that swooped lower than Sarah would ever dare, and painted lips and cheeks. One woman caught her eye, the pale long slope of her neck as perfect as any portrait Sarah had ever seen, and a small heat built in her stomach. But she wasn't here to admire. Another yelp came from above, where the bedrooms were, and she started up the stairs just as a man wearing less clothing than he should started down, grumbling about the noise and a refund.

A familiar shadow appeared in the doorway to the kitchen and followed after her. Sarah refused to turn around until she'd reached the top.

"There are many other midwives in London," she said. "Many closer, too, and many who were not sound asleep, I'm sure."

Margaret wiped her hands on the dish towel she held and then tucked the cloth into her back pocket. She wore a man's breeches and boots, which as always looked far too fine for what Sarah guessed her salary was. This was a nice brothel that cared for its staff, but a serving girl made a pittance in every house in the kingdom. Today, she had a long scarf wrapped around her head, in a Moorish style from the Continent. It hid what lay beneath quite well, though it could hardly help her blend in at all.

"Do you dislike money?" Margaret asked. "I can't imagine

your mistress gives you anything equal to her cut of the commissions. Perhaps midwives take a vow of poverty as the nuns do?"

"I'm paid well enough." Sarah felt unaccountably irritable. It was too late at night to match barbs with a brothel's sharp-witted kitchen girl. Yes, the lateness of the hour, that was it.

Margaret shrugged. "You did well the last time. The girls trust you."

Sarah was fairly certain that the girls did not even know her name, given that the last time she had only arrived when the laboring woman was well into the worst of the pains, and none of the other painted ladies had bothered to ask. The madam had simply leaned into the room when it was over, seen the squalling infant, sighed, and handed Sarah a handful of coins that seemed scrounged up from the cashbox. She'd had to spend that bit of money carefully, else Mrs. June would ask where she got it. There was nothing particularly wrong with having harlots in your clientele, but Mrs. June dreamed of working for a certain strata of society and none of these women were expecting to become the kept mistresses of dukes or barons. A silk trader's wife would be intrigued by using the same midwife as an earl's kept woman, but she would disdain the midwife on retainer to the brothel her own husband favored.

She found the laboring woman in the first bedroom, and checked under her skirt before the other girl holding a damp towel to the back of her neck could question her. "She's almost here—you should have called me sooner."

"They were going to try to do it themselves," Margaret said. "The madam'll take your pay out of her cut."

The baby's head came and the rest of it swiftly after. An easy birth, all said. She would never encourage a woman to try it alone—that was bad for her business as much as for their health—but this one could have managed had she waited half an hour more. She prescribed hot wine with slurry, and told the woman she could take the baby to her sister's—a chandler's wife—when he was three days old.

"Should've called them sooner," said her friend. "Might've avoided the whole business."

The woman was recovering herself as rapidly as she'd given birth. "I wanted to know what it was like."

"And now it'll be a month before you can work and *ech,* you won't like eating porridge that long."

"Women have had babies for many worse reasons," Sarah provided, and they both looked at her with what seemed a truly ungrateful measure of annoyance. The door behind them—not quite latched—creaked open and the matriarch of the house leaned in as she had before and handed Margaret some pennies while Sarah cleaned her hands.

Margaret let the coins slip from one hand to the other. "Enough here for a pint."

"I'll have more work in the morning. I should sleep for it."

A young boy edged into the room. One of the other

women's children maybe, now employed to keep things tidy. Margaret pointed toward the basin with the afterbirth and the dirty rags and he gathered them up while he rubbed the sleepiness from his eyes. Sarah gave her address to the mother in case there were complications, but she was already drifting into a heavy doze and her friend shooed them out. Plenty of mothers here to mentor her if something did go amiss, and Margaret had made it very apparent that she knew where to find her.

"A pint," Margaret said again.

"I'm very tired."

"I don't understand your reluctance to get to know each other." Margaret touched her temple, hidden under the scarf. "Surely not for these, when you yourself—"

"I have a reputation to maintain."

"Does it tarnish a midwife's reputation to aid a birth?"

That wasn't what she meant, and they both knew it, but if she acknowledged her true meaning, she'd be giving in.

Sarah had tried so hard in London to be respectable. Out of fear at first—she had given in to her desires and her darkness in Cookham, and look where it had gotten her, and she could not risk Mrs. June turning her out. But six months in, she saw, like a distant street lantern shining through the fog, a future she desperately wanted and might someday have within her grasp. A profession that would bring security, and a mistress who might, someday, if Sarah tried hard enough, treat her like a beloved daughter. Whenever Mrs. June said, *Yes, like that, very well done,* she felt that thing she was not used to—pride—twist inside her painfully. She prayed desperately some nights not to disappoint.

Yes, she had tried to bury her desires beneath pride in her work and fear of the poorhouse. But here she was, still their creature.

"A pint," Margaret said a third time with a smile, and held out her open palm full of Sarah's pay. Sarah snatched the coins away and their hands touched—Margaret's was calloused and warm.

"I think I shall buy myself one," Sarah said. "And I suppose I cannot stop you following."

The streets were quiet this time of night, though many workmen were pulling themselves grumbling from their beds by now. Margaret led her down an alley to a pub that was barely more than an overhang no one had claimed before, with a crude lion's head sign hung askew. Sarah bought herself a cup of mum from the sour-faced woman standing over the barrels. She preferred it to beer for the herbal taste, though it was rarer these days. Even with the fire, the air chilled her. Margaret pulled close so the heat rose off her woolen cloak and stuck to Sarah's skin. This was much like the night they had met, though that had been late summer, and the air hazy with the smoke from fireworks instead of fog. Sarah had been in the city only a month then, and the strange births had only begun. She had looked across a narrow street and seen Margaret, and been struck with that fresh bolt of recognition that Mrs. June was teaching her to cultivate, the same one she felt when she came to a birthing bed and knew the baby would be born uncanny.

Or maybe that moment, too, had only been desire. She found the feeling of her own wants hard to tell apart from her sense for witchery, sometimes. Both were cool, sharp needles in her.

"You could have called someone closer," Sarah said, and tried not to sound whiny.

"I was bored," Margaret said. "It's quite boring in a brothel, if you're not one of the ones being bedded. I think Madame Charpentier is disappointed in me, you know. I think she hoped I would grow into an exotic delight when she bought me from my parents. But I haven't the taste for her clientele."

Sarah, in all these months, had not asked the name of the house, and now she frowned at it. "Charpentier? She isn't French."

"No," Margaret agreed. "But better advertising than Jane Small's House of Delights, eh?" In the thick folds of fabric between them, she touched the back of Sarah's hand. Sarah fumbled the drink in her other hand, the wooden cup suddenly far too slick. In Cookham, she had not been a woman who fumbled things.

"I don't know why you persist in this pursuit," Sarah said, though she did not pull away. She lifted her cup and the mum went down bitter in the back of her throat, having grown too warm in her grip.

"You never want for someone like yourself?" Margaret shifted back against the brick wall, letting the January chill rush in to fill what had been the warm space between their bodies. "For . . . an understanding?"

Sarah hoped the darkness hid her pink cheeks. She didn't need to ask if Margaret meant their shared uncanniness or their shared desires or the shared danger either of those put them in. She meant it all. That September day, when they had locked eyes in the midst of the drunken crowd, Margaret had simply crossed over, leaned close, and said, *I sense you are like me.* It was a festival, everyone was doing what they shouldn't, and so hidden behind a stable Sarah had pressed her mouth against Margaret's neck. Margaret was wearing a dress and bonnet that day, and when she undid the bonnet strings, her hair fell around two small, curling horns. And in that single frozen second, Sarah saw the fear cross her face, fear that she had mistaken what Sarah was. But Sarah had only frozen out of recognition, and a stranger, deeper longing; a hollow sadness that with a sharp knife her grandmother had removed her only uncanny mark. She hadn't realized she held that ache, for a body where she could be seen and known at once.

A strand of dark hair had come undone from beneath

Margaret's cap. The other occupants of the pub were all too drunk to pay attention to them. Sarah reached up and tucked it back under the band, and let her fingers touch the place where the horn connected to Margaret's skull, that seam of skin and bone. The first time Margaret had called her to a birth as a pretense, she'd left as soon as the baby was out. There'd been no chance for conversation. Lingering here was a terribly thoughtless mistake.

"You've never shown me your mark," Margaret said. Her voice was heavy with desire, but Sarah thought of the small, faded scar on her back and that unfamiliar sorrow struck again.

She dropped her hand. "My mistress will be up soon. It's been a long night." She left her cup and made for the street, even though Margaret's footsteps followed close behind. She thought about calling for a cab with the rest of tonight's payment, but no, there would come a day when she needed to hang her own shingle and she could add this to the pouch hidden beneath her mattress.

"I did not mean to push too far." Margaret stopped four paces behind her, and this distance between them told Sarah that Margaret had misunderstood. Sarah was no stranger to women's touch. Before marrying Michael, she'd had plenty of both men and women, in that fumbling way that young people did behind hay bales or hidden in a hedgerow. If she allowed herself, she could leave

Margaret gasping into a pillow, begging her to stay. But she did not know how to explain the ways that they were not alike.

"I'm only tired," Sarah repeated, and left her standing at the edge of the gutter.

CHAPTER 5

That Wednesday, the Wrens sent a hackney cab to collect Sarah and Mrs. June. This was not so unusual for their wealthier clients, but a treat enough that Sarah found her best working dress and scrubbed her face and hands hard. Mrs. June packed little treats that she usually did not give away for free—a tea for nausea, a sachet for swollen feet to put in the bath, a few honey candies rolled in nuts. Faith Wren was not the wealthiest client they had had, but Sarah didn't need Mrs. June to tell her that the intangible quality of *fashion* could be worth so much more than a noble title or a family fortune. It was a different age from the age that Mrs. June's own mistress had grown up in. These days, men wanted their sons to be astronomers and doctors, and women wanted their daughters to know beauty and culture instead of only silence and skill. The return of the monarchy had brought a new age. The gray Puritan mood had lifted with Cromwell's execution.

The Wrens' home had beauty, but not the kind Sarah

was used to. Yes, they had some of the fine markings of wealth—tapestries on the walls and carpets underfoot, staff, portraits of the family on the walls. But there were also strange devices—sundials near every window, compasses, atlases. This was how a man of science lived, she supposed. A maidservant whisked them efficiently up to Lady Faith's rooms before she could take in much more.

Stranger still, Sir Christopher met them with his wife.

Usually, husbands attended their wives' appointments only to haggle over the cost of their services. Sarah saw Mrs. June take in their surroundings—the well-stocked firewood, the maids hurrying about, the clean clothes—and then Wren's presence, debating whether their client's husband had suddenly lost their wealth in a bet, as was apt to happen, or whether he was just stingy.

"Please do go ahead," Wren said. He sat at the edge of the room, with a portable desk and inkpot. Faith sat in a chair, embroidering a whitework design on the edge of an underskirt. They looked a matched set, him with pen and her with needle. Perhaps she was as odd as he and simply hid it better. "I only plan to observe."

Mrs. June looked at Faith, who smiled indulgently and set her stitching aside.

"Perhaps you would enjoy a cup of wine in your study instead, sir?" Mrs. June asked. "There really is no reason to bother yourself with this business."

"On the contrary, I think it may be illuminating."

"Go on, you won't get rid of him." Faith got up and propped herself up on the bed. Mrs. June gave Sarah a shove forward—whether because this had been her acquaintance or because Mrs. June was still disconcerted by a husband in the room was unclear. She started the examination. The baby was much as she had perceived the first time she had felt it. Nearly ready to come. She waited to be rocked on her feet again, but it didn't happen—she felt the sharp connection, an awareness of the baby's unseemliness that seemed to vibrate in her like a plucked fiddle string. But it did not overwhelm her. Sir Christopher sat in his chair and sketched, and sometimes asked her or Faith some question about the structure of the feminine parts that often neither of them could answer. Sarah had been up close with dozens of bodies and what she could say was they came in a great variety; she was not a surgeon to philosophize on the inner structures. At one point, Wren made her stop for a good several minutes while he held forth on the work of a Dutchman who discovered eggs in a woman's ovaries and theorized that this was the source of generation, rather than a man's seed.

At this, Faith sighed and drew a woolen throw over her bare legs, tapping her stockinged foot against the bedpost as he carried on. When he finally finished with an explanation of the Latin roots of the word *ovum,* she just tilted her head up to the embroidered canopy and said, "Can you imagine, Mrs. Davis? The idea that men would be responsible for generation when it is so clearly women who must always bear the brunt of the work."

"As it is in most things," Sarah said. Mrs. June's eye twitched—she'd get an earful later, but Lady Faith laughed and her husband merely looked indulgently aggrieved.

"Yes, very put upon, womankind." Sir Christopher had sketched in his pages a section of his wife's anatomy, and not for the first time during this visit, Sarah wondered if there was something else a little untoward going on here. Men and women exchanged scandalous pictures all the time, and someone had to model for them surely, but Sir Christopher did not seem the type to sell his wife's nether regions for a shilling and Lady Faith hardly seemed the type to sit for it. "In fact—several of the ancients wrote that it is impossible for women to get pleasure from the act of copulation. Perhaps I should stop trying so hard, Faith?"

Mrs. June made a sound like a carriage axle breaking. Faith just snorted and patted the hill of her stomach. "Not trying much at all, currently, are ye?"

"Now then," Sarah said, because she did not know what else to do. "I think you'll be seeing this baby before much longer, my lady."

She knew it for a fact, actually. She felt it deep in the marrow of her bones. This boy would be born on a day as gray and heavy as wet wool fresh off the sheep, a day that threatened rain and snow in equal parts and cared not at all for human comfort. She could not see how he would look—she wondered momentarily if Mrs. June could, and then decided she couldn't, not with how she reacted sometimes to the ones that came out strange. She stood up sharply, to hide the sudden pain that lanced through her lower back. A deep, dark unease settled in the low pit of her stomach, and when she looked at Mrs. June and Sir Christopher, neither of their faces helped ease it.

Perhaps she ought to try to get Faith alone, to warn her. Were there likely to be other complications, the mother would be warned. But how to name a thing like this? And she could think of no way to separate Lady Faith from her husband.

It was only a baby, she told herself, no matter how it came out. It would live or it would die, it would look perfectly human or it would look uncanny like the others, the world would expand to hold it or the Wrens would do like other couples threatened by scandal.

Just like that, her own mother's voice came to her clear as a bell, *I should have drowned you, all the trouble you've caused me.* And then the image of Michael striding into the river like he was expecting God to make him a fish and let him breathe in it.

There were a few more questions for Faith, and Mrs. June let her take them. Had she felt the baby quicken? Yes, yes, she had. Had any physical ailments particularly bothered her? No, the nausea had been better than with her first pregnancy, and the pains far between. Mrs. June ordered hot compresses for the muscle strains. There was a strange air in this house that Sarah did not care for, but whether it was a deeper sense from her uncanny half or just the oddness of Wren's papers about the marital room (anatomical diagrams, alchemical recipes, a small model with many gears that she could not begin to guess the purpose of) she could not say. Since her first encounter with Faith, she had been filled with a low, buzzing unease, like there was a great beast approaching, dragging its massive body over the earth, and churning dirt and people and churches and homes beneath its uncaring bulk. She could feel its massive bones and hot, acrid breath; she could see it coming like a sailor could see the storms before the clouds gathered on the horizon. The world would be all ablaze soon; soon there would not be a world like this at all.

Sarah gasped and the cold air shocked her back to the Wrens' bedroom. Sir Christopher was pulling the bell to summon the serving girl—the fire in the hearth had burned low. Her head was full of the end of the world. Or perhaps the end of the world was inside her, incubating, waiting to burst free of her warmth like an egg cracking after tender love from a mother hen.

"Yes," she said, though her hands shook. "Not much longer yet at all. A few weeks, I would say." Mrs. June nodded in agreement.

"And what is the likelihood, do you think, that the child will be born healthy and hale?" Sir Christopher asked. He looked up from his paper and smiled politely, like he was asking a common question about swollen feet or childbed fever.

Mrs. June answered for her. "That's in the hands of God, sir. I have no way of knowing. If only we did. A birth defect has numerous causes—some even come only on the eve of birth, if the babe can't breathe quick enough. Surely you know this yourself. I understand you are very accomplished in the study of medicine."

"And surely you know it is not the common deformities I speak of." Sir Christopher touched the back of Faith's hand, lightly, even as she cast him a reproachful glance. "The coffeehouses are full of it, but the Royal Society's study has been limited. Men of my circles are not much allowed in the birthing room. I would very much like to see one of these for myself, but all considered, I would prefer it not be my own."

Mrs. June did not repeat that it was in the hands of God. How could she—this was obviously a matter beyond God, or sideways to Him. "I am afraid that if the midwives of London knew anything more than the Royal Society does, we would have shared it. Of course we do not have your university training—our expertise is limited to what we have observed in the course of our own apprenticeships and what other midwives are able to pass on. Surely there is nothing we could know that you do not."

Lies—there were many things that a laboring mother was willing to share with her midwife and not with her husband. This polite denial of their own abilities was just another curtain drawn between the sitting room and the birthing room, the male sphere and the female sphere, and like all the other divisions it was mostly invisible until invoked. Wren knew it, too—Sarah saw the moment when he decided that Mrs. June was not worth further questioning. He gave her the thin, patronizing smile that the man of the house gives a new servant whose name he cannot be bothered to remember, and fixed his attention instead on Sarah. She felt the weight of it settle on her. What must it be to be one of the corpses his ilk took apart with their scalpels. She could feel herself being stripped down, skin peeled back, and muscle expertly flayed from bone while the etcher sat in a corner and recorded accurately the pieces of her. She bent over the bed to avoid his gaze and helped Faith up.

"All's in order," she said. The lie tasted like meat gone rotten in summer. "A few weeks."

"We'll send for your mother," Wren said, the first normal comment Sarah had heard him make. "Better to make the trip early, in this weather. Mrs. Davis, you will be attending primarily?"

"Mrs. Davis is my apprentice." Again, Mrs. June answered before Sarah could, and she had to bite down on her tongue to stop herself from saying anything rash. "I will be overseeing."

"It is Mrs. Davis who assisted Faith today, and therefore

I would prefer her attending." It was his money, and he had enough of it to insist on almost any concession he wanted from them. But this was unusual enough—especially from a husband—that Mrs. June bristled at it.

"I would not let her attend any birth alone. That's simply unwise. Far too much potential for mistakes."

Mrs. June was right to protest, but Sarah still flinched at the dismissal of her skills. Then she saw Wren watching her face and tried to school it into professional stillness. He rubbed at his mustache, like he was thinking it over. "Surely her skills could not be so lacking. Have you let an incompetent apprentice use your name?"

"She's known the trade six months. Would you trust a six-month-trained farrier to shoe your stallion?" Mrs. June snorted like it was the funniest joke she'd heard all winter.

"Very well," Wren said. "You will both attend, then. Now—shall we discuss your preferences for payment?"

Later, when they left the Wrens' home, Sarah found herself in a storming mood, the sort that would lead to a lightning strike sooner or later. Mrs. June noticed, too, for she huffed a little on the way home and bought them both a too-expensive late winter apple from a stall.

Sarah weighed the apple in her hand and felt it too light an offering. "I wish you had not made him doubt my skills."

Mrs. June sank her teeth into her apple and the softening skin gave with a wet pop. "It is *my* name your work reflects on now, and don't you forget it. While you are my apprentice, it is your duty to bolster my reputation, not to build your own over mine. Someday you shall have your license, and shall feed yourself by the strength of your own name, and then you can call yourself the best midwife on all the isle for all I care. Until then—do not try to over-shadow me in front of our patrons."

Sarah nodded. Mrs. June seemed satisfied, but the apple tasted bitter, like it had sat long enough in the cellars to start to sour.

Not even the oddness of the king's surveyor could cloud Mrs. June's joy at the commission, and as a reward for orchestrating it, she gave Sarah a few pennies from her purse and allowed her an evening to herself. Sarah found a woman hawking roasted eels and bought one for more than she would usually stand for. She picked the meat from the little bones while standing on the street corner near one of the worse pubs in this parish, where no one would bother her. The eel was mediocre, overcooked. She twisted one of the rib bones free of the spine and used it to clean a sticking bit of the flesh from between her teeth.

So many if-onlys. If only this were a different world. If only she had been born the kind of man rich enough to buy respectability or noble enough to demand it. If only she were a different woman, who did not desire so strongly so many wrong things.

"Mrs. Davis."

She startled out of her reverie. It wasn't so late but the sun had already long vanished. She squinted into the dark and saw a man in clothes too nice for these streets standing in the shadow of a Hungarian coach.

"Sir Christopher." She should have been surprised, but somehow it was the least surprising aspect of this entire day. The low simmering rage in her belly flared hot, and she sucked the last bit of oily meat from the eel's spine to give herself an excuse for a pause. "Is there a problem? Has Lady Faith gone into labor?" Too early for that—there'd been no sign of it this morning.

He shook his head. She could tell only by how his shadow shifted.

"I made some inquiries." His voice was mild. It drifted alone with the cool night breeze like a part of the air itself. She could imagine him teaching students at Oxford with this voice, softly trying to needle something out of them without them realizing it at all. The last bit of eel meat went down sticky in her throat and with a gurgle from her stomach. She wiped her greasy fingers on the front of her apron. He had followed her here—this was not a street where men like him came, with the unswept coffeehouses and pockmarked eel sellers who were clearly selling yesterday's catch. There were a few possibilities, and she liked none of them. "Faith was happy to rely on Mistress June's references, but I preferred to be thorough and check your reputation as well. The last midwife was, after all, such a disappointment."

"It's admirable that you care so deeply for Lady Faith."

He inclined his head. She did not like that she found him so difficult to read. She had met men of science—it was a particular favorite of the lesser nobles and the upper classes who strove to affect the new look of respectability—but this was not an affect of the field. He came out of the darkness and offered her his arm; she had little choice but to take it. They carried on at an unhurried pace not toward the Wrens' home but toward the lodgings she shared with Mrs. June. Another small bit of leverage for him to wield—*I know where you live.*

"Drowning is a dreadful way to go." His hand rested lightly on her, and he shortened his steps so she did not have to hurry to keep up with her smaller legs and more cumbersome dress. She resented the consideration. "I worked with the body of a man taken from the Thames some time ago. The way the lungs looked—quite painful. The rivers were bad last year with all the rain. Even people who had grown up around the rivers and should have known them lost their footing. My cousin lost his youngest son to the creek he had played in every day of his life."

"Yes. It was a wet spring." Michael's face came to her, that sallow, blank expression he had worn just before his head had disappeared beneath the churning murk. She thought, sometimes, that she had seen his hands clench before he went under, like he was fighting whatever spell had taken him. But she hoped that was merely something her mind had made up from the guilt. She would never be sure, she knew. She would wonder about it for the rest of the time she walked the earth.

"When I wrote to your village reverend to ask about you, he told me you had left quite abruptly after your husband's death, even though you had a family whose home you could have returned to. Plenty of brothers, he said, and enough money to keep you even if it would have been tight. He said you were leaving ahead of unkind gossip, though he was too dignified to tell me what that gossip was."

All technically true and yet, not true at all. Sarah did not relax. They walked on. A drunkard leaning against a signpost shouted something incoherent at them, probably a comment on an aspect of Sarah's anatomy. Wren gave him a sharp look and the man returned to conversing with his ale instead.

"Of course, the nice thing about the darkest gossip is there's always an old woman with nothing better to do than talk your ear off about it. For free, even." He laughed suddenly and Sarah jumped. "And your mistress seemed so surprised when I asked what you knew about the babies. Women talk, and there are some things women will talk about only with other women, but then, they do talk so very much."

She would not bite her tongue for him. Not when Mrs. June wasn't here to disapprove of it. "And what is it men do in coffeehouses, sir?"

"Are you a witch, Mrs. Davis?"

She forced herself not to stumble. He seemed prepared to stop for her, and surprised when she did not. She did not know if he took that as any evidence of her guilt. She glanced around them, but there was no one close enough to hear—it was late enough into a chill evening that most everyone wanted to be home by the hearth, drinking or working or fucking the cold away. London was not a little village where the whispers could carry end to end as fast as they were uttered. And this was not the time of James I, when the paranoia had run the country like a plague, the hangings as regular as the notches on a sundial. The courts were no longer convicting on the word of children or lunatics, the way they'd convicted the Pendle women a generation ago, all eight of them hung by the neck until they were nothing but dead flesh and a cautionary tale.

"Let us turn this way," Sir Christopher said, and touched her—two fingers pressing lightly on her elbow, so respectable—to guide her to the left. "I do know the value of my patronage. To you and your mistress. I would like to hear how events unfolded, in Cookham. I give you my word as a gentleman I shall not use it against you."

How events unfolded. What a gentle and inadequate

summation. To tell it true would be to tie the noose around her own neck. And yet she looked into his earnest eyes and began to tell the tale.

An interlude in Cookham,
and the terrible event there

She had not meant to kill him. She may have been—may still be, even, much as she tried to be anything else—brusque and unkind and too easily tempted by the fickleness of her own desires, but she had never truly wanted anyone dead before. She had lived with Michael for six months at that point, washing his clothes and cooking his meals and enduring his long, cold silences. The truth was, he was as unhappy with her as she was with him. They were ill-suited, opposite tempered. He did not really want a companion; he wanted a cheerful maid to neaten up his life while he spent his time plowing and planting. She did not really want a husband to bend herself to; she wanted to be away from her parents' home and the ever-empty bowls and her mother's sharp tongue. They talked over each other. He seemed to find every small thing that annoyed her to make a habit of. She found his obligatory attempts at affection clumsy at best, and laughed at him when he tried to kiss her on the cheek or hold her hand. She couldn't help it. And when she laughed at him, he turned mean, sulking in a black mood until the ale loosened his tongue enough for him to tell her she was a frigid woman, incapable of either love or, barring that, wifely obedience, or on the worse days, that she was a demon sent from Hell to torment him. She laughed at that last one, too—again she could not help it, she had not been raised with kindness and found it by nature hard to mimic.

She did not have it the worst. One of her school friends, Charlotte, was married off too young to an older man from the next town over after her father fell into ruinous debt, and that man was cruel with his fists as well as his words. At least when she failed to live up to what a wife should be, she had to pay only in time spent listening to Michael's prattling on. And yet she could not stomach it. She tried to imagine herself ten years on, with a baby on her lap, still mending shirts and listening to him drunk in the corner mumbling that her stitches weren't small enough. This was what she really couldn't stomach—he lied. She'd had the neatest embroidery of any of her sisters, and she knew her mending was nearly invisible. She could take an honest barb, she could not accept one that was a lie.

Slowly they stewed in their cool dislike of each other, until it festered into a quiet, constant hatred. When they went to church on Sundays, their bodies leaned unconsciously away from each other until the old widows who sat up front added it to the gossip that cycled around the town square. Sarah also took to ale, let it give her enough false courage to tell him she wished to be a widow, so she could have money of her own and no husband in her bed. He had laughed and told her to try poisoning him, then, though she had better succeed, for if she didn't, he would have her hung.

The rains came that fall and the river flooded its banks. The current turned from placid to whitecapped; a boy downriver drowned trying to save his toy boat from the shallows. Swept away in an instant, bloated body appearing three days later downriver yet farther, full of holes from small things with teeth that lived in the current.

It was one of their short-lived truces. They tried to be like other couples and take a stroll down the bank. Michael offered his arm and Sarah accepted. They stood up on a knoll and watched the swollen river carry away a leaf, a rotted wagon wheel, a whole log as wide around as a man.

"Do you truly hate me?" Michael asked. He had not yet been drinking. Sometimes she thought he might be simple.

"I don't hate you," Sarah had said, though without any affection. She'd had a headache all day. Strange dreams had plagued her, full of shadows and a bleak, gray world where monsters lurked, and ever since waking, the light had hurt her eyes. She did not want to have to pretend to love him again. For one, she didn't mean it, and for another, she never played the part convincingly. Her back tingled, and turned to a sharp pain at the scar where her grandmother had stripped her of her unseemly tail. "I simply wish I were not burdened with you."

He breathed in sharply. She hadn't meant to say that. It was too much. Her head had grown light, like she might faint. She pressed her hands against her eyes.

Her tongue moved of its own accord. "Do I have to hate you to wish you dead? Your death would free me. I wish you would throw yourself in the river, under a cart, whatever is quickest for you to let me be."

Sparks lit behind her eyes, her head and scar throbbed, the pain growing and growing until she thought she might scream. She heard Michael's footsteps receding. She thought he'd left her, and the anger welled up again to match the pain. The anger sharpened that pain into a knife. She felt it heavy in her hands, as heavy as the cleaver she used to butcher chickens for the pot. She imagined using it on him and for a moment relief flooded in. She imagined being free of him, and the headache broke like a thread snapping under tension.

She opened her eyes.

Michael hadn't left her. He was picking his way down the path, toward the river. Mud sucked at his feet, but he didn't slip. He moved like a man who longed for the water.

She thought about calling after him. She could've—she had to admit that to herself, later. There was a second where she could have called him back. But she did not. And he did not look back. He stepped into the river like he expected it to be dry land, and then he was gone.

They pulled his body from the river that evening. He

hadn't gone far at all, not even to the next village. The shirt she'd mended last week had caught on a branch where the river crooked near the Haverfords' land. When they brought him to her, his face was the most peaceful she'd ever seen it.

She told everyone it was an accident. She had thought she would be free. But two of the old women from church had seen them, it seemed, first their conversation and then Michael's calm procession into the water. It was too inexplicable. They said that she had said something—and she remembered the feeling of her mouth forming words, though she could not remember what they had been— and then he had turned with the eyes of the possessed and drowned himself. She had just stood there, they said, no screaming or begging, not even surprise. This was also the truth. She remembered watching it, though it had felt like watching through someone else's eyes. And oh, she remembered *wanting* it. That was the part the old women did not know and the one she could never speak of—she wanted to be free of him, and for that, he had to be dead, and so she wanted him dead. It was the most she had ever wanted anything up to that point. It had taken her over and the power that lived in her had made it so. She did not need anyone else's whispers to know the truth. She hadn't asked for it—not consciously, she was no murderess at heart— but in that moment, her conscious will was worth nothing.

There was not enough there for a mob to run her up a gallows right away, but the rumors of witchcraft and murder started that night and built and built until she had no choice but to leave. Only luck had sent Mrs. June to her before she left on her own.

When she had gone to say goodbye, her youngest sister sat by the fire and would not speak to her. Her mother chopped carrots at the table, each strike of the knife shaking the board.

"I found you a decent man," her mother said, and shook her head, like this was all to be expected.

"I didn't kill him," Sarah protested, though it wasn't true.

"*Pfah.*" Her mother brought the knife down again and the top of the carrot jumped and rolled away across the floor. "You drove him to it, if you didn't bewitch him. Go on, then. You haven't anything left to linger for here."

And so she took the only open door she had left, the one offered by Mrs. June, who held the only key to it and never let her forget that fact. Sometimes in life God gave you only a single path, and one must walk it or perish by the flame or the noose. Sometimes she lay awake with the noise of the city outside the shutters, trying to fit within a life unlike any she had ever prayed for, and knew the Sarah Davis of Cookham had died in the river, too.

"Here we are," Wren said, abruptly, cutting off the musing end of her story. Sarah stumbled over a loose stone in the street and looked up. She'd lost her sense of herself in the telling.

The Monument rose above them, the scaffolding on its unfinished column reaching up like bare branches tangled among each other. Wren took an iron key from inside his coat and went to a small door that had escaped her notice upon her first visit.

"I believe your tale," he said. "And I appreciate your entrusting it to me. Now, if you would trust me once more."

He opened the door. And perhaps he, too, had the witching blood, for she followed him down the small staircase there without thought to her reputation or her safety. When they emerged, they were in a tight room, three meters a side perhaps. Wren lit a candle on the table in the center.

The candle guttered in the draft from the window and Sarah itched to go and fix the shutters tighter. Wren scratched at his chin thoughtfully. She was well aware now, as she had not been in some weeks, of the differences in their stations, him knighted and the Surveyor of the King's Works, her an apprentice midwife with a black cloud of suspicion following her like a sickening miasma. She did not belong in this place, among his books and dials and pendulums. "When I was at Wadham," Wren said, and it took her a long moment to remember that as the name of one of the colleges in Oxfordshire, "they hanged a maidservant for killing her baby. It was one of the most fascinating things I saw during my studies. Unmarried, you see. A bastard. It was quite the scandal. No—that was not the fascinating bit—after they cut her down, she was set for the dissection table, but when they opened the coffin to begin the study of her anatomy, we saw her breath still moving in her, and the anatomists revived her. Can you imagine? To be hanged as a murderer, and then to have life returned to you through chance and the providence of the right man of science being at hand?"

She forced herself to smile rather than shudder at the implication of her reputation resting in the hands of this right man of science. "You have a very gentle way with threats."

Wren startled. "A threat? No, I merely—don't you think that interesting? It was just what came to mind."

Sarah searched his face and if there was malice there, he hid beneath an unreproachable veneer of respectability. "Very well," she said. "Do lead on."

He led her beneath the monument, down a dark and winding staircase bent inside the great column. Inside the stonework, the cold fingers of the late January chill released their grip and the feeling slowly returned to Sarah's frozen hands. Wren set his candle on a table spread with papers and strange mechanical objects, and went to light the hearth. Sarah went to the table while he stirred the catching coals with a poker. Some of the articles she was familiar with—descriptions of new scientific discoveries from the London papers, written in the vernacular for people like her. Most of the rest were in Latin, and though she had a word or two of that from anatomical studies, most of it was beyond her. She recognized sketches of celestial bodies, perfect in their overlapping orbits, and astrological drawings of the Greek constellations. A model pendulum weighed down a stack of unbound mathematical pages, still wrapped in the bookseller's blank vellum. She set the pendulum swinging and watched it arc ever smaller.

"Another fascinating thing," Wren said, and she looked up to see him watching her from the fire, even as he continued to stoke it higher. She could barely see anything in the underground gloom, but just then, the fire took and her breath caught. The room was so much larger than she had imagined—she could see this table replicated sixfold, the space stuffed to brimming with books and arcane objects in various stages of assembly and disassembly. "There is some invisible force that draws the bob back down. Many in the Royal Society favor the idea that we are surrounded by aether, and it is collisions with these small particles that leads all momentum to eventually stop, and holds us to the earth. Although my dear friend Hooke believes that the planet itself—all bodies, actually, though it is only noticeable with the largest—exerts a great attractive force. Quite the debate a few years ago."

The fire lit and roaring, he crossed over to a shelf at the far side of the room and rustled in the papers until he found a print. He held it up and Sarah recoiled at the horrid creature, many-legged and covered in small scales and smaller hair drawn to look stiff as wires.

"A mite," Wren said. "They live on every inch of you, especially the hair and eyelashes. Very, very tiny. Only visible with perfectly crafted lenses. There is a whole world many times smaller than our eyes can perceive. It's possible this small world is even responsible for many diseases. Tiny organisms invade our bodies like an army invades a foreign nation." He thought over that metaphor and chuckled. "Or—I suppose it would be more accurate to say like the Catholics threaten to invade the Houses of Parliament. A much quieter invasion."

When he turned his back again, Sarah touched her eyelashes and tried to feel something wriggling there. Nothing. If they were that small, she supposed she wouldn't feel them at all. Somehow the thought was not particularly comforting. She'd seen lice aplenty, crawling over the heads of everyone in London without the time or inclination to comb them out. She just had not imagined similar crawling things so close to her eyes. "Surely you did not bring me here to frighten me with pictures of invisible beasts." He had to be aware as much as she was that they were a man and a woman unrelated and alone together in the dead of night. Her widowhood and his marriage would protect their propriety only so far. Though it was only her reputation at stake—there was no such thing as a fallen man, and this was not France, where mistresses enjoyed good society and only fashionable scandal.

Once again, she felt herself standing on the surface of a lake in early spring, ice melting, disaster a misstep away.

"Once the monument is completed, I intend to use this as a laboratory. Experiments in pendulums, particularly. But that isn't the only reason I built it into the plans." Wren lifted his lamp again to light the far wall. The largest map of the city of London that Sarah had ever seen was pasted up there, as tall and wide as she was. Someone had carefully marked different points with pins. Many of the pins were clustered in areas that had been decimated by the Great Fire, and were even now only skeletons of what they had been. Rebuilding was slow in the best of times, and these were hardly the best of times, with everyone holding their breath for another rebellion, another plague.

She supposed they did have another plague, just not the dying kind everyone had expected.

"London is one of the oldest still-inhabited cities in the world," Wren said. He gestured at the Thames, where it crossed by the city walls. "The Romans built it. Can you imagine? This city is older than Christ Himself." He seemed to get off track—she could tell there was a tangent he wanted to barrel toward, but he pulled himself together and pointed at the pins instead. "Many of these streets and buildings have been here—in more or less the same place, even if their function and form have changed—since Lon-

don's earliest days as a city. Until the fire, that is. Now—
what do you call it, again?"

"London?" she asked, confused.

"No, the—" He waved his hand, and not for the first
time Sarah thought that Faith must be a woman of infinite
patience. "The source of your witchcraft."

An icy chill settled in her stomach and her legs tingled
with the desire to run. But there was no use denying it, and
also nowhere in London where this man could not find her.

"We call it the Other Place." One secret revealed. Her
mouth went dry, as if Mrs. June might be listening.

"Yes. The well of monstrousness and magic. I propose
that what your society calls *the Other Place* is actually a
separate celestial sphere. Perhaps the opposite of ours, with
aether taking the place of matter, and matter of aether. But
I digress—the exact physics of it remain purely theoreti-
cal." He paused. "Do you understand, essentially, what the
study of physics is?"

"Yes." She heard the knife's edge in her own voice and
winced at it.

"Hmm." Wren examined her again, in that way that
made her feel like a specimen pinned to a board, or worse,
like one of the unclaimed corpses destined to be cut to
pieces and drawn up in someone's anatomy book. "Pity
you're not a man, isn't it? You might have done quite well—
Hooke didn't come from a notable family, and look at his
contributions." Before Sarah could think up a response,

he jabbed again at the map. Damn him. She'd never had anyone knock her speechless quite so often before, and she found she didn't care for it. For all her sharp tongue got her smacks from her mother's wooden spoon or Mrs. June's open hand, she liked having it as a weapon when it was needed. "I propose that there is a magnetism between this world and the Other Place—or, as I have come to call it, the Sphere of Aether. Certain points of geography repel each other, like magnets with their poles aligned. Thus, the gravity of our sphere and that other sphere attract each other, while the points repel, and we are held in harmonic stasis. It is the same as the forces that keep the moon tethered to us, without bringing it crashing down upon all our heads."

"And the specific geography of London is one of those points." She saw where he was headed. The first rumors of monstrous births had appeared in the year after the last rubble from the fire was pulled down. The oldest unseemly child she had seen herself had been seven years or so. A boy begging in the street, his mouth covered in a handkerchief. Some older children being cruel to the less fortunate had run by and yanked it off, and screamed when they saw he had not one mouth but two, one with sharp teeth on the left side of his face, and its mirror on the right side with teeth that were sharper still. He'd dropped his money and run, smart lad. A few pence wasn't worth a mob after you. "The fire destroyed . . . the magnet's poles. And now instead of being kept apart, we are drawn together."

"Exactly. I believe there has always been some amount of overlap—else how would some alchemical feats, which otherwise confound the laws of nature, be possible? But it was limited and controlled. I have been attempting, in my role as Surveyor of the King's Works, to rebalance. But we are still being drawn closer every moment."

"Surely London can't be the only pole. It is old, but it isn't eternal. And one city cannot possibly balance the world."

"There were many great old cities in the Americas that the Spanish destroyed in their conquests. It seems likely some of them were also poles. And we live in an age of great wars—cities burning across the globe—the city of London may have just been the last point to fall before the structure itself gave way." He drew another large sheet from a drawer in the desk. An illustration of the celestial bodies, the stars and moon and sun, and other bodies that Sarah did not recognize, until she leaned in to read the label and discovered that they were other planets, spinning their own circles out there somewhere in the dark heavens. The illustration had been done so that each body had a double of itself, a shadow, trailing slightly behind. "We believe now that the arrangements of the heavenly bodies are not constant but shift over ages. What may have been a strong alignment when the universe was created has come askew. And so my efforts to rebuild the city are insufficient."

Sarah looked at the moon on the illustration, leashed to the earth. She thought of it crumpling, the great devastation it would wreak if it ever fell, crushing people and cities and entire countries beneath its great weight. She did not need Wren to explain to her the even mightier devastation that would come if the Other Place spun even farther off its axis and broke through the barrier between their world and its dark nonsense. A globe sat in a stand in front of the map; she set it spinning with the lightest touch and stopped it with a finger on England. "How do we put it back?"

"Well." Wren sighed at the map. "That, unfortunately, was where I was hoping for your assistance."

"I am afraid I am no great scientist. If the Royal Society doesn't know how to turn it back—"

"This is a matter beyond science." Something changed in Wren's gaze. Instead of the unfocused, fluttering fancy he'd had before, he stared directly at her. "My society has occasionally dabbled in the alchemical arts. To no great success, I'm afraid. But I understand that your—I believe I hear you call it a *guild*"—he looked at her, and she tried not to hear mockery there—"has worked with much more success with the powers of the Sphere of Aether."

"The midwives of London have not received royal permission to form a guild," Sarah said as if that were the only objectionable point. But there were strict penalties for forming a guild without the king's approval.

"Let us do away with obfuscation. I am a careful listener, and many people who are not used to being listened to speak too freely. I learned of your society when I took up my post—at the time, I only thought your magic village superstition."

Sarah flinched at *village superstition* and the image it conjured of old women warding themselves against her in Cookham. Wren softened. He spun the globe and it whispered on the axis, countries and mountains and oceans blurring into one another. All gone if someone did not rebalance the world. "I think—if we use the example of magnetism, even if the exact properties do not align—that it will take a great force to set things right. I can theorize—"

"You do little else with your time, it seems." It slipped out before she could resist the urge to try to cut him.

He either did not hear or found it funny. "I can theorize, but I have no power in that realm. You and yours, it seems, can move between here and there. I think with the proper timing, geography, and force, you can set the spheres in parallel once more. Geography I have in hand—the Monument was built on the weakest point between and should provide a door. Timing, well, I think we both know we are accelerating toward a day of reckoning, and the calculations there should be straightforward now that the speed of acceleration is visible. That leaves force, and for that I also need your assistance, as I cannot observe what factors act successfully upon that sphere."

"I see."

It wasn't the way she would have chosen to describe the Other Place and its workings upon the earth, but when she lined up his words and hers, she could see that the logic was the same. Mrs. June would disapprove. For many reasons. But it did not seem she had a better choice. She spun the globe again, and in the candlelight, the strange countries that she would never get to visit seemed to flicker and merge, becoming stranger lands still. She wondered if the lands of the Other Place matched, if there was an England there, with a king and wars and laws and colonies.

"Help me," Wren said. "We can turn the world back toward the face of God and His natural order. Imagine a world where crops that flourished last year do not fail the next, where we can predict killing frosts as easily as we know the boiling point of water, where children don't die mysteriously of fevers." His voice caught. So there it was—a son buried, a father desperate.

"I will tell you all I can." Not a promise, not quite, but the potential of a partnership. She pretended not to notice the wet gleam in his eye and turned toward a pointed pendulum to allow him to collect himself. She, too, wished for a different world, after all.

In the early morning some two weeks after Sarah's association with Wren began, she woke early to go for cheese and bread for the week. Usually a morning walk without Mrs. June cleared her head as well as a draught of the cleanest, crispest spring water; today in the weak morning light, she was only cold and annoyed at the damp. Spring was far enough away to be little more than a dream. And spring, of course, would be only a few weeks of fragile bliss until the summer came and with it the heat and the stinking rot of the waste left in the streets and washed by the cartful into the stagnant, swelling Thames. Back in Cookham, they at least had open fields and woods to get away from the stink of humanity. She missed so few things about that place, but the open space was one of them. Here you could not escape from the crush of so many bodies stacked upon one another.

She was so engrossed in thinking about the creek she played in as a child, with its muddy eddies and sweet, clean water, that she almost did not notice the shadow stalking her.

When she did notice, there was no ignoring it. She caught it because its shape was so wrong. Not the blocky shape of a cart or building, or the expected animals (cattle, horses, dogs). This was large and furred and it moved with a sloughing, rolling motion, like the way the gelatin from boiled bones trembled after it set. She stopped, and the strange shadow became indeed just the outline of a cart piled high with hay. What strange pictures one's mind could make when left alone with its follies.

Still—her hands were damp with sweat suddenly. She tucked them inside her cloak and decided it was best to turn back. She left the water and the fishermen hawking the first of this season's catches, and cut down an alley overshadowed with crisscrossing clotheslines hung with moldering washing.

It was much darker in the alley than she had thought. But still, it was morning and this was a decent part of the city and though she was a woman alone, she had never looked an easy target.

Then, she smelled it. Sour. Bitter. Not rot—oil? Char?

Tallow rendering. That was the smell. But she didn't know of a chandler down this way.

She tripped on someone's discarded table scraps, and when she picked herself up, she saw it.

At first, all she knew was a hulking mass of black fur that shivered and shimmied like strands of kelp. She stuffed her fist in her mouth to muffle a scream, because the only thing she could think was that she had finally gone mad. The fur shuddered, and what must be arms emerged—a wrong number of arms, and all of them waving desperately at her. She staggered back, and slipped on those same traitorous potato peels, and fell backward into the muck.

The beast approached. The air around it seemed wrong; it made Sarah's skin prickle and her teeth hurt down into their roots.

It stopped at her feet. Two slit nostrils the size of her hand flared under the fur. Its body writhed again and she could not tell—was that it preparing to attack? Or, no— she saw it now, in the way it seemed bent under its own weight—that writhing was agony, twisting every muscle and nerve.

Then it opened the mouth she had not known it had. And inside, in two neat rows, were teeth just like a person's. Molars, canines, incisors, just like she had seen in the open panting mouth of every woman whose baby she had ever delivered. Only these were small and very white, just like milk teeth.

She wanted to scream again, but for a different reason.

She had not thought that, just as there were children here born partly of the Other Place, there might be children *there* born partly of the earth.

And this one had . . . fallen through the thin division somehow? The way the air warped like its body did not fit in this reality—

It must have smelled her own strange unseemliness, and thought her one of its own. Shame and want welled up inside her, and she shoved them down as soon as they came.

She reached out her hand. It flinched, but did not run.

"You need my help," she whispered. It startled away and she froze.

It opened its mouth. What came out were not words. She didn't know why she had expected words. This noise was . . . locusts, on top of someone smashing a tin cup against a table over and over.

She clambered to her feet. This time it didn't flinch. She had to fix this—Mrs. June might know how to bend the worlds enough to open a door, even if she could not do it herself. But the sun was rising, and the people were emerging from their houses, and how could you hide something like this through the streets of London? Maybe—she did not know how to do this either, but the idea was so appealing she kept turning it over in her head—she could bring it to Wren, and it could teach them how to bridge the worlds and stabilize them. She thought of Mrs. June's patronizing smile, her smirk when Wren had praised her steady hands. Yes, Wren would help, and be pleased to do it. Not only that, he would be ecstatic to have another object of study.

"Ho!"

Both she and the creature jumped. The contents of a chamber pot splashed out a third-story window and Sarah wrenched back to avoid it. The creature howled—shocked, afraid—and its outline shimmered.

"Wait!" Sarah said, but it was too late and it didn't understand. It fled back down the alley and when Sarah followed she found only an empty street with too many shadows and crannies to search.

CHAPTER 6

Another night, more pebbles tossed like hail against the shutters. Pure luck that Mrs. June was out tonight dealing with a breech birth that would take until morning if the baby lived, and longer still if it did not. Sarah was making tea by the light of a precious beeswax candle, but she took the kettle off and threw open the shutters.

"Come out with me," Margaret said, from below. "Six months in London, I am sure you've not seen all of its joys yet."

Sarah could have made many excuses—there were clothes to be prepared for their great wash on Sunday, mending to be done, letters from another midwife in Germany that Mrs. June had deemed educational and added to her list of reading. But it was also an unseasonably warm night, and as she leaned out the door, she heard men laughing, and a woman cackle with joy, and well, what harm could there be in one night in London? She got her tippet and mittens, and tied her pocket on, and then followed Margaret out into the night.

They did not call a hackney cab. Sarah thought perhaps it was for money, or perhaps because Margaret's boyish look stood up to the soft light of the streetlamp but not to the scrutiny of a cab driver. They kept walking, beyond the walls binding the city, to a parish that respectable young women were not supposed to frequent. They were near to the theaters, but these streets lacked the carefully culti-vated debauchery of the theater district. The men here were much drunker, the inns much more crowded (doss houses, really, if she were being truthful rather than charitable), many of the women displayed a wanton bit of lace at cuff or ankle that indicated their affections could be negotiated for. One of those women caught Margaret's eye as they passed, and then Sarah's in turn, and gave them both a knowing smile that turned Sarah's blood hot.

They came to a tavern with a sign showing a red-maned lion whose gaudy paint was slowly peeling in the damp. Margaret swung the door open and passed through the bar, through a crowd of rowdy men deep into their tan-kards and gambling on a pair of fighting cocks in the cor-ner. It was a mixed crowd, Sarah noted, some dressed very fine, and some who likely were spending their last pennies. Margaret knocked on another door at the back, said some-thing to whoever was beyond, and it opened for them.

Back here were more tables, though crowded closer

together. A pot of sack posset bubbled over the smaller hearth and the smell alone—wine, clove, milk, and egg—went straight to Sarah's head. The tobacco smoke hanging low in the air gave everything the hazy quality of an early-morning dream, before the bellboy came around to yell the hour. Margaret ordered them cider, though it seemed most others in the room were already into the posset.

A lithe young man lounging in one of the faded chairs uncurled himself, and when he came over to them, Sarah saw his face was painted like the wanton woman's outside, rouged cheeks and a blush on his lips. "Margaret!" he said. An actor? No—his clothes were too bright and revealing even for that profession. A mollie boy? Sarah had read the scandalous lines in the papers, of course, but given her own inclinations and clientele, she'd never had occasion to meet one of the boy whores favored by a certain subset of the wealthy men of London. "It's been awhile."

"I've been busy," Margaret said. She kissed the man's hand, like a gentleman might a lady he grew up close as kin with. "And did not want to spend all my hard-earned coin on a single night's debauchery, as I tend to do in your company. Martin, this is Sarah."

Sarah had been looking around the room, now seeing which men were mollie boys and which were the men who slept with them, which seemed to be couples of two men or two women sitting close as lovers, a few women even dressed as Margaret was. She jumped at her name.

Martin smiled kindly, which she bristled at before she saw that he didn't mean to patronize. "Margaret, you do so like to shock your friends. We take to tribades here as well as we do to sodomites, my dear."

"Martin is one of my oldest friends." Margaret took a long drink from her tankard. "He used to be a servant at Madame Charpentier's house as well."

"Took to the actual work better than Margaret here did and make a fair penny more now."

"Only because they don't set up whorehouses for women," Margaret said, and they both laughed the way one does at an old and many-layered joke. Sarah sat next to them and drank her cider until the tankard was empty, and with that warm fuzziness settled in her stomach, the gay atmosphere took hold. Someone struck up a fiddle and she danced with a blackamoor woman in a stunning red bodice, and a Scottish girl in the plainest serving-girl hand-downs. She drank a cup of sack posset and threw her pennies for it to the harried tavern girl, and let the hot wine turn her vision swimming. Margaret introduced her to an older woman ("the first friend like me I met, when I was old enough") and a tall woman named Bess who, upon a further look, her parents had probably thought a son upon her birth ("Would you prefer to be a man?" Sarah asked, thinking that there was a message behind the introduction. Margaret shook her head. "There's a difference between the dress of a thing and being it."). Martin told a joke about one of his patrons that not even the bawdiest broadsides would dare to set to print, and Sarah found herself racked with the most unladylike laughter, bent doubled over another tankard of cider until she cried.

The night grew old, and most of the patrons began filtering home or to the relative privacy of one of the inns along the street. Martin drained his last cup and smacked the tankard down on the table.

"The last shows will be letting out," he said. "I'll have a friend or two waiting for me."

"See you soon," Margaret said, and he kissed her cheek as a brother would, and then she and Sarah were alone together at the table.

"I did not know places like this existed," Sarah said.

"I'm glad you enjoyed yourself." Margaret's words rolled easily out of her mouth, but the wave of drunkenness had passed over them both and left only a pleasant intoxication. She lifted her near-empty cup and considered something. "I thought you might think yourself above it. Above . . . other people like us."

"I don't—that isn't what I've ever meant."

Margaret looked at her silently.

"I am nearly alone in this city. If I lose Mistress June's favor and am turned out—" Sarah lifted her hands. She could not even speak it. She could not return to Cookham, no one else would employ her without a reference, and she was not pretty enough to make a living as Martin did. The edge between a good life and starvation was as thin as a silk thread. "I am glad to have found myself in a respectable occupation, that allows me some freedom and money of my own. But that isn't the whole of it."

Margaret sighed, but it was a sigh for the state of the world, and not for Sarah. "I know."

Sarah looked into the fire, and in her ale-addled head it seemed like a portal to a different kind of life. "Someday—when I have established my own name—"

"That sounds like a start of a promise, and a promise is a strong thing to give a woman you've spent only a handful of nights with."

Sarah kissed her. Margaret returned it and for a second Sarah could hear nothing, see nothing, all her senses had narrowed down to the ale-sweet taste of her. Margaret took her hands and brought her to her feet, and led her out the back door of the tavern. They were in a quiet, dark alley. The door closed on the laughter inside and turned it to a dull murmur, a light, happy tune in the background. A streetlamp glowed warm at the far end of the alley, but no one could see them from the street. Sarah wanted unnamable things so desperately that her mouth had gone dry for desire of them.

Margaret slid a cool hand up her leg, above her stocking, to where the wool knit met her wanting flesh and let the touch linger there.

"Please," Sarah said as she pressed her mouth to Margaret's neck, the sliver of skin above her collar, the soft spot under her chin. Margaret swallowed and the shudder of it made Sarah bold. Margaret abandoned her cassock, and Sarah helped her to free her shirt from her trousers. The ale must have made her bolder still. She kissed Margaret's bare stomach and then cupped her small breast, and felt with no small amount of satisfaction and shock and swift hot desire how Margaret's nipple went firm under her touch.

Margaret kissed her on the mouth again—bit her lip—and then that hand underneath Sarah's skirts and smock went higher still and stole whatever Sarah meant to say next. This cursed shirt—she wanted to take Margaret's breast in her mouth, kiss her all the places so cruelly covered by lockram and muslin.

"You should—" Margaret said, and swallowed again. "Let me—" Her hand moved up some more and Sarah leaned into the touch. "Do you want—"

"Please," Sarah said again, though how Margaret understood that needful sound that tore out of her throat, she didn't know. Her fingernails scraped down Margaret's back, and Margaret's breath came hard and fast. She'd seen plenty of fucking—nine babies in her family after all, that wasn't for want of sex—had plenty of it herself, plenty of the shouting, moaning kind, but this time she couldn't make a sound, because she wanted to hear Margaret's heart thudding against her ribs, wanted to memorize the sour-salt-spice taste of her mouth and the calluses on her hand as they felt her wetness. For this one liminal moment, they existed only for each other. Margaret's fingers slipped inside her and Sarah gasped.

Sparks burst deep in her stomach—she closed her eyes and reached for Margaret, reached for that humming sensation that felt like it wanted to burst from her skull. When she blinked, they weren't pressed up against a brick wall anymore but floating in another sky. Stars in green and puce and whelk blue shimmered all around them. Then the wave of pleasure crested, and that humming power slipped out of Sarah's grasp, and they were back in the London night, breathing hard against each other's skin. Margaret's hands trembled against the small of Sarah's back and the scar there, and Sarah held her breath.

"I've done this a lot of times," Margaret said, her lips still only the width of a hair away from Sarah's bare collarbone. "But you're the first one who's ever had tricks like that."

Sarah tried to get herself together; her legs shivered and her hair had come out of all its pins. "Surely you have the talent for it, too. Manipulating the Other Place. Don't you feel it about you?"

The shadows hid Margaret's eyes. She wiped her hand on her trousers and tucked her shirttail back in. "Aye, I feel it. Once when I was a girl, a man tried to cut my purse at the market and I got so angry that I cut the hand from him instead. Fell from his arm like they'd never been joined. But that was the only time. Can't do it on command, like your lot can."

"It's mostly training. You could be trained."

Margaret laughed and pointed to her head. "Some of us are taken for talent and some of us are taken for oddity. What respectable midwife would take on one as marked as me? Yours is hidden, whatever it is."

"A tail," Sarah said, her tongue loosened by the wine and the pleasure and the desire to give Margaret something in return for what had been given to her. "But it was cut from me. I wonder—your horns—"

"I wouldn't do it," Margaret said. "Even if that were within the surgeons' power. It's shaped me too much. You shouldn't give up the things that made you." She fit her hand into Sarah's again. They leaned against each other at the edge of the streetlamp's glow. Sarah wanted to ask what that made her, if the mark that should have been part of her life had been taken. Did she belong to this joyous, uncanny world of mollie boys and trousered women, or did she belong to Mrs. June's world of respectability and rules? Or perhaps, was she forever split between the two, too un-canny for good London society but without the mark that would let these ones trust her? Though most of these people were not marked as Margaret was. Desire, she knew, was a different thing from the strange power inside her.

Margaret tilted her head against Sarah's shoulder and

the light caught her eyes, heavy-lidded from the ale. "I did not mean to make you melancholy."

"Most things make me melancholy," Sarah said.

"I've noticed that." Margaret kissed her cheek, the lightest comfort.

"Do you ever—" Sarah said, but the question was hard to form; she so rarely had occasion to talk like this, with someone who might understand. "See it, reach for it, the Other Place? That faraway place that feeds us. You could change the shape of this one."

Margaret was quiet. Her breath steamed. Her thumb rubbed back and forth over Sarah's knuckles, they were damp with each other. "I dream of it sometimes. A nonsense land, overlaid on ours." She paused and then the smile was back. "But I like my pleasures warm and ale-soaked; I wouldn't twist this world to fit me better."

Sarah leaned into her again, close enough for a kiss, close enough for a secret. "Sometimes I would. I think— what has this world ever been to me? What wrack and ruin I could bring. I could—"

A movement on the main street. A scraping sound, like a drunk dragging himself home or something large shuffling along among the muck. They both froze, waiting for a shadow to cross the streetlamp, but it never did. The ale-warmth had fled with the startle; Margaret squeezed her hand again. "Shall I return you home before your mistress wakes and starts worrying over your honor?"

"Luckily, being a widow does provide some protection from my reputation being ruined by a notorious rake."

Margaret laughed at that, and heat that couldn't be blamed on a good drink flared in Sarah's belly. The whole walk home, strange constellations danced behind her eyes.

CHAPTER 7

Shocking, how easy it was to work Sir Christopher and his laboratory into her routine over the weeks that followed. Once or twice, he called for her with some manufactured concern about Faith's condition, but most of the time she simply devised it so Mrs. June was out on an afternoon when she had no chores and slipped away. She stopped going to the tavern much, and turned down the other apprentices the few times they deigned to ask her. She did not crave their company anymore, or the scraps of friendship they occasionally saw fit to give her despite her uncanniness. If Sir Christopher whispered about her and whether or not she was a demon, he did it outside of her company, and that was all she asked.

And the *laboratory*. She luxuriated in the laboratory. The odd mechanics, and the small jars of chemicals, and the books of alchemy and mathematics. She always spent the first length of his company wandering from wall to wall asking, *What is that? Or that?* And Wren named them for her: an armillary sphere to represent celestial distances; a treatise on the circulation of the blood, which discredited the theory of humors; a set of lenses that turned very tiny creatures large enough to see. Even if she were a boy, she would never have been of the class to be an Oxford man, but she could imagine that life so vividly that it seemed sometimes to be a divine vision.

Over the weeks, they had gotten closer to what Wren called *a unified theory of the balance of the worlds,* created out of his geographical and chronological calculations, and her refining of different esoteric writings until she hit upon a wording that seemed to resonate with the power inside her, a choir in harmony. Now they were nearly there—the date of the collision pinned down to the nearest week, the spell and symbols writ in parchment, and Faith's pregnancy nearing its end.

"Read it once more," Wren said. He leaned back in the drafting chair, his shirtsleeves rolled up to midforearm. They'd stoked the fire up too high and now the room was all smoke and heat, and a line of gray sweat dampened his collar. The hour grew late; soon Mrs. June would come back from her house call.

Sarah took up her slate and began reading the text they'd compiled from Dee and Jabir and other mystics. She began reciting the cant, and her skin prickled with it. She felt like the words were sharpening the power inside her, as a blacksmith's hammer turns a lump of red iron into a spear point.

Sometimes on the return walk, she would try some small magic—turn an apple in a passing cart rotten, crack a cobblestone down the middle—and it would come as easily as breathing, no effort at all. The effect never lasted, but on that walk, she understood what lords and kings might feel, to have the world bend to them with a word and not a drop of sweat.

The wind picked up. The room hummed like a choir warming to a song, many throats coming into tune. The plank ceiling above shimmered, like lips glistening, a mouth threatening to open. Wren leaned forward and the fire caught his eyes and made them bottomless. He'd taught her the sounds of the Latin and not the meaning, but that didn't matter when she could feel the power building inside her with every ancient syllable.

Sarah hit the last line, careened toward the last words, stopped. For a second, the stone walls still trembled. And then the room became once more just a room, the world once more only singular.

Sarah laid the pages down. Her hands trembled but it was only because her heart felt like a caged songbird that had finally found the aviary door open. Wren smiled at her and she stood a little straighter to be the perfect image of a successful experiment.

"Not so long now," he said. He stood, took the pages, made a minute correction that she would see next time. The small grate up high on the wall to let in the light had turned dusky gray; she would be late getting back. She gathered up her things. "One more moment, Mrs. Davis."

"Of course."

"Your mistress said you could not tell when a child would be born strange," he said. "Was that true? Odd— your profession is so quick to judge a child a girl or a boy, fair or dark."

"We're not always right on those."

"That is an answer to a different question."

Mrs. June would murder her for telling him their secrets. It was one of the great unspoken rules—some things were the domain of midwives, and ought to stay that way, both for the protection of their business and for the protection of women's secrets. And while there were some men, she knew, who could access the Other Place, it was the midwives who had banded together as a profession to discover and document its workings and pass down their teachings. She had no assurances that Wren would not turn around and publish everything she told him for every learned man in Europe to use in his alchemical laboratory.

And yet: she thought of how they had spoken once and he had immediately deemed her not only intelligent but an authority on a matter that he was not. And even when he said, *Pity you're not a man,* it was clear that what he meant was that there were some things the world would not allow her, some heights she could never see purely because of the accident of her birth, and he wished it were not so. She had not known she wanted this so badly—someone to see her potential, and also to understand that she could never reach it, and what a sadness that was.

She discovered she wanted to live up to his expectation.

"We can," she said. "I can't prove it to you. I can sense it, the way I sense the Oth—the Sphere of Aether."

He did not seem surprised. "And my child?"

She hesitated, but nothing in him read like anger or fear. "Strange," she said.

He rubbed his beard. His mouth twisted and she took a step back, just in case he was the sort of person whose anger erupted like a pot boiling over when you lifted the lid, but nothing came. "Don't tell Faith. Not in her delicate state."

"She will see it certainly."

"Yes, but she can be spared the anticipation."

It was against what she stood for. Yes, sometimes the truth should be smoothed over, like telling Rebecca her son had merely been born wrong, instead of strange. But you did not leave a woman unprepared. She paused, and then saw that trust in his eyes start to slip. He did know his wife better than she did. Perhaps she would prefer to not know until the birth. "Yes. All right."

Sarah let herself back into her rooms as quietly as she could, but her hands shook and the key jangled in the lock. She held her breath and listened—nothing. The windows were

dark. And there were no women due this week for their errand boys to have awakened Mrs. June. She eased the door
open and slipped into the darkness.

"Out late, my dear?"

Sarah jumped. Mrs. June's voice came from near the
hearth, but the fire had burned down so low that Sarah
couldn't see her even when she peered into the warm haze.
An ember popped and she tried not to startle. The February chill had invaded the shutters and the rooms weren't
warm enough now to keep her from shivering. She came
close, with the excuse of feeding the fire, and there was
Mrs. June, sitting up next to her writing desk. "Only to
the privy."

"A good walk this time of night."

Sarah stirred the embers and the fire grew. Her cheeks
had gone numb on the long way back and now they burned
when the heat touched them. "My apologies if I disturbed
you returning. I could not wait for morning."

"Are you thankful to me, Sarah, for keeping you from
the noose or the pyre?"

Sarah held herself very still, even as the smoke got in her
eyes and made them sting and run. "Of course, missus."

"Then I hope you are only fucking him. Because surely
you are too grateful to me to destroy everything I have
worked for so long."

The edge in Mrs. June's voice sliced right through Sarah's middle, and she bit back a little gasp at the sudden

sharp pain as her stomach twisted over on itself in fear. She clenched the poker in her hand, and forced herself to prod a red-glowing coal that disintegrated at the touch from the iron. "I would never do anything to cast a shadow on your reputation."

Mrs. June tapped her fingers on the table like she was thinking, but Sarah knew that drumbeat, and knew it was actually Mrs. June restraining herself. She stood up, and turned to her mistress. She readied herself for a sharp smack across the face—Mrs. June was quick to that, when she thought Sarah was edging across the boundaries of respectability set for her as a widow and a midwife—but it didn't come. Instead Mrs. June stood and turned away from her. The air hummed. Mrs. June was reaching into the Other Place, holding what power she could draw from it in her hands. This, somehow, was more frightening, as much as Sarah knew she could draw down more power if she wanted to. But she couldn't, that was the problem— Mrs. June was right, she owed her everything she had, and could not bring herself to raise a hand against her bene-factor.

"Do you think you are the first young woman to find yourself in this position? With a man above you telling you that you are special, impressive, powerful, and he needs you to give him everything you have?" Mrs. June picked up a book off her desk—one of the midwifery manuals she had had delivered from the Continent. She smacked it against her other open palm, once, twice, the sound like a hand on actual flesh and not just leather and paper, and Sarah winced in time with it. "And how many fellows of the Royal Society have been hung for witches or stoned until they were dead? Who is the one gambling here? Mark my word—you will come out of this association with your reputation in tatters at best, and at worst, a charred corpse or a monster twisted by powers beyond your control. That is the way of this world. You have something that man cannot buy with all his money and influence, and so he has seized it by propping up your fragile ego and telling you that you are special in a way no other touched maiden in the world has ever been. The thinnest lie in the world, but you want it so badly, you stupid girl."

That old rage fizzed in Sarah's chest. She had spent so long ignoring it, cooling it, shoving it deep inside her where it died for lack of air, and she had thought herself finally free of it. But here it was again, the tongue that would destroy her, the anger that she would burn herself down with. "I do not know what you are accusing me of. I think you envy me, that this power is a part of me when you can only touch it and wish for it. I spoke true—I would never harm you or your reputation. And I *am* grateful to you for this new life. But you do not own my life. Let us understand each other on that."

Muscles jumped in Mrs. June's jaw. The fury inside Sarah deserted her, but she could not give ground now.

Where she had expected to find anger in Mrs. June's eyes, she saw instead only a shallow disappointment.

"Very well," Mrs. June said. "Go to bed, then. Plenty of mending to do tomorrow."

"Yes, missus," Sarah said, but her mistress did not even wave her off, and a cold beyond the winter night settled around her again.

CHAPTER 8

The headiness of a battle won lasted until the next time they met with the guild. Mrs. June had been sour-faced all week, snapping at Sarah for stoking the fire too much or too little, for not packing her bag fast enough, and for generally being a disappointment and a waste of her investment. Sarah had weathered enough bad days before. She bowed her head and followed orders.

Then they arrived at the tavern and Sarah saw the new apprentice.

Good thing they paid the tavernkeeper's wife double to clear the room for their meetings. This girl must have to veil her face in polite company. Thick, coarse fur like a goat's covered the left side, and that eyelid slumped toward the cheek, tugged the wrong way by the strange structure of her bones. She looked from one midwife to the other with a mix of terror and pride.

"Where did you find her, Judith?" Mrs. June asked.

Mrs. Evans smiled. "Spain. All papists down there, you

know, blabbering on about witchcraft and heretics, they were more than happy to give her to my man. And she is very happy to do as I ask."

Mrs. June's eyes slid to Sarah, but Sarah refused to look ashamed. Let them think her ungrateful. She would save them all with Sir Christopher, on her own terms, while they prattled about in their secret societies with their old books and mystic ramblings. "Well. We must have options. Things are progressing too rapidly for delay."

"The worlds shall tear each other apart," said Mrs. Weatherby, an old, old woman who sat in the corner at these meetings and never seemed to take an apprentice of her own. "We have come to the time of Revelations."

Mrs. Evans and Mrs. June rolled their eyes together. Mrs. George's apprentice, the strange boy, stretched uncomfortably in his chair. What an odd one. Sarah wondered if his former alchemist master had taught him something of celestial mechanics before turning him out.

"Three strange babies in three days," Mrs. George said. "And all of them dead. Revelations or not, this must be put to an end."

Mrs. Evans opened her birthing bag and began to take from it an array of items: a good knife, a lead plate, a book of symbols, an extravagant spring-balance watch wrapped carefully in cloth. Close to the tools that she and Wren had struck upon in their experiments. So they and the guild had worked toward the same solution, after all. But the guild did not understand the importance of geography, and timing. One needed a telescope for that, and no one in this company was wealthy enough. Sarah looked at the goat-faced girl and thought about saying so, but no—Wren had confidence in her, more than Mrs. June had ever displayed, and she would not break that. Let them fail and draw up nothing more than some sad fizzled magics.

"It's an auspicious night," Mrs. June said to her, quietly. It *was* auspicious. The sky was clear, the air sang with late-season ice crystals, and someone had reported a meteor shining overhead in the early evening. But what Mrs. June meant was, *Will you let her apprentice succeed instead of you, and shame me?* And Sarah found that yes, she would; she had no desire anymore to be a tool for her mistress's reputation. Let Mrs. June turn her out. She had clients now. She could survive. And Sir Christopher would help her, she was sure. He had been so unfailingly kind to her. She said nothing, and turned her face away.

She knew what they wanted—they wanted a door. All these women had spent years with the smallest taste of power, knowing that there was so much more of it to be had in a world just beyond their own. Did they think they could take it, if they just found a way to the Other Place?

Mrs. Evans spoke to the goat-faced girl in clumsy Spanish. The girl understood well enough. She stood on the symbol drawn in the center of the floor and began to read.

The air in the tavern room shifted. All the warmth fled.

Sarah could see that the others felt it—the boy appren-tice shivered—but where they could merely reach for this power, it was a part of her blood and bones. And those bones were now vibrating inside her flesh.

"This seems an ill omen," she said. Her tongue was thick in her mouth.

"Oh, shut up, girl." Mrs. June's eyes were glued to the sacrificial apprentice. "You had your chance."

"You don't know what you're doing." It came out scratched, her throat closing on itself.

Mrs. Evans laughed at her. No kindness in it at all. "Of course we know what we're doing. The barriers between the worlds have gone soft. It brings to us monsters and chaos, and if we do nothing, we will all be torn apart. We shall bring the Other Place to us instead—let everyone partake of its magics."

The goat-faced girl kept reading. A great creaking sounded, like the whole world was being rent open. The tavern shuddered, and one of the other apprentices screamed. Sarah looked up—a great maw had opened in the ceiling. No, that was not quite correct—a great maw had opened in the place in the world where the timber ceiling should be. Instead, they all gazed upward at wrong stars. Sarah trembled. The air heaved with the power of that Other Place. So *much* power. Her hands trembled. That power whispered to her uncanny blood, told her she could be a queen of queens if she took it. And Sarah almost did. But the chord it struck in her felt wrong.

The goat-faced girl stumbled over her words, but kept going.

They had it wrong—the wrong geometry, the wrong geography, a door opening to an ocean instead of the providence of dry land. They wanted to remake the world and fill themselves with the power they coveted—but it was not as simple as that. This power could not be molded so easily.

One of the apprentices—Anne, with the safflower hair and the greedy eyes—reached for that power in the air. She didn't need to move but each of them with the sense for it saw her do it all the same. She tried for it and the weight fell upon her and she crumpled moaning to the floor. Her friend Thea tried to help her up, and when she did, they all saw that one of her eyes had turned to a gray sphere of lead.

Mrs. June hesitated. But it was too late. The other world had found the goat-faced girl and now she was locked to it. She wasn't quite here anymore—or quite there—through her skirts and bodice and skin Sarah could see her bones and the circulation of uncanny humors. She held her breath. This may work. The guild may get the world they wanted.

But no—the air heaved again. The alignment was wrong. The goat-faced girl's mouth opened in a scream but all the sound fled up to those strange stars.

"Stop this." Mrs. June grabbed Mrs. Evans's wrist. "She isn't prepared, clearly."

That wasn't the problem, but they could not know that. Sarah tried to see if there was some way to step in, but she and Wren had not explored how to end the bridging, only start it.

The sky cracked. The strange stars flared like guttering candles. The room itself seemed to shriek in rending pain. Sarah covered her ears, closed her eyes, tried to concentrate on the ground beneath her feet in the hopes that it would not betray her.

And then, it was over. Sarah opened her eyes, the lids gritty like she'd slept in the blink between. The room was as it had been.

The goat-faced girl lay on the floor. Some of her bones were where the skin should be and vice versa. She had no face anymore, just one featureless plane of coarse fur. Shockingly, there was no blood.

Mrs. June clutched Sarah's arm. Sarah yanked herself free. "So this is what you'd see done to me," she said.

She should have expected the smack, but she didn't, and it came sharp as a newly honed knife. Her ear rang from the force of a blow.

"You stupid girl," Mrs. June hissed. "Is this what you have for me, spite? After all I have done for you? This is the culmination of generations. That girl is dead. And all you can see is yourself. Get out, then, and leave us to this mess. Back to our rooms. Get out. I can't stand the sight of you."

Sarah wanted to scream at her, scream at her for the dead girl and the ruined ritual and that dark empty chasm inside her that would still like nothing more than to make Mrs. June proud of her. But she knew what came of opening her mouth in times like these. Her future hung by a thread and Mrs. June held the scissors to cut it. So she turned and left the tavern and the guild, and held her head high like she could be certain she was right.

CHAPTER 9

For the next two days, Sarah and Mrs. June moved in silence around each other as the two spheres did, unable to leave each other's orbit, unable to bridge the empty space between. Sarah had braced herself; she could see in every pinching muscle in Mrs. June's face that she wished to dismiss her rebellious apprentice, but her uncanniness was too valuable now, too singular.

On the evening of the second day, when Sarah was trying to find words that were not just the same argument in a different order, the Wrens' kitchen boy came pounding on the door to tell them Lady Faith was in labor.

Mrs. June took up her bag and jerked her head to Sarah— she was too necessary for this, too.

As soon as Sarah's feet left the doorstep, she knew something was wrong in the city. A winter night like this, a storm in the air, most people would be huddled in their homes or in the alehouse. But the night was full of distant shouts and clangs in every direction, and the whole of the city smelled like a bonfire.

Mrs. June felt the wrongness, too. She held up her hand; Sarah stopped short. "Boy. What's happened?"

The kitchen boy laughed. He was young enough to find everything new exciting. For some reason, it turned Sarah's stomach, and the smell of the air gave her a queasy headache. "A terrible crime's been committed. Everyone's turned out to string up the devil responsible." That was hardly an explanation—it was midwinter, the city was bored enough to make a mob for the slightest counterfeiter—but he seemed to remember his laboring mistress and darted off toward St. Paul's. Sarah and Mrs. June had no choice but to follow, but as soon as they turned from their small lane onto the market street, they were met by a crush of people, shouting and screaming. Sarah stopped short and in that one instant she lost both Mrs. June and the kitchen boy.

She tried to shove her way through the crowd. Someone jeered—someone else's hand cupped her bosom, but jerked away before she could be offended—someone else stepped on her foot so hard she shouted and the crowd thankfully, blissfully, parted enough to give her a few seconds' breath. A man with a rake over his shoulder howled up at the sky like an unchained dog, and the man beside him, who was far too well dressed to be any compatriot of the first, laughed like they had been friends forever. It was a festival air, a rioting air, an air that ended with drunken brawls or drunken stampedes or the king's men driving everyone drunkenly back to their homes on horseback. Except there was no festival today, and in the smoke she smelled not gunpowder but burning meat.

"Let me through!" she shouted, for all the good it did. "I am a midwife, and there's a baby to be born!"

A group of women in front of her parted some, but as she passed, one of them said, "Pity that, born a little too early, when we're to slay the beast!"

"What?" Sarah rounded on her, even as she caught sight of Mrs. June forging ahead.

The woman grinned and swayed. Based on the dress she wore, with its fashionable square cut that showed her shoulders, she was likely a merchant's wife. Too rich for a crowd like this usually. She pointed toward the center of the crowd, where the fire burned. The smoke got in Sarah's eyes and stung them too teary to see through. A dark shape loomed up on a pike, carried by a man covered in something equally dark and oily and smelling like fat.

"Came to a fishwife to turn her baby," said another woman, this one dressed like the first's maid. She had a harelip and chewed unconsciously at the twist in her upper lip. Her breath was very fast. Excited. "Her husband saw it, gave chase. Did you not hear the news being shouted?"

"When we chased it," said the first woman, though she was not out of breath in the slightest and so Sarah doubted

112

very much that she had chased anything more than a bit of good fun, "it ran right back to its mistress. A witch! A witch in London, with the mark of the Devil upon her! They have her in Newgate, but you believe me, soon as the sun rises, we'll try her by water. Can't let this kind see a court."

"You're a midwife, you say?" said the second. In the light from the burning torches, her face was cast as a skull and her eyes gleamed out of bony sockets like every badly printed broadside's version of a devil. "You'll be gladder still of this! An end to what's plaguing our babes. No more monsters for women to look upon and have imprinted upon the walls of their wombs, after we kill the witch and her hellbeast."

Everything she'd eaten for supper curdled in Sarah's stomach. Mrs. June had managed to find a break in the mob and was headed toward the Wrens' home, but Sarah turned from her and pressed instead toward the fire and the smell of scorched hair. A man laughed at her and splashed warm wine over her shoes—she flinched back and ran into another with a look in his eye that she didn't like at all. With every breath, she tasted someone else's sweat and it built up in the back of her throat and choked her.

She finally made it to the center of the crowd. A group of men held the pike, and others—other men, women, children—were pitching stones at the bloody thing skewered there. Each one hit with a deep, wet noise, and blood spattered into the fire and hissed. She wiped her eyes but still could not see.

"You want a look, miss?" One of the men saw her and grinned. He was drunk as anything, a miracle that he was on his feet. He grabbed her arm and dragged her forward out of the crush of screaming people. She stumbled onto a crate—almost into the fire—and then she was nose to nose with it.

It was the creature from the docks—the *child* of that Other Place—who had come to her for help, who had seen her for what she was.

Or at least its head.

Sarah screamed.

The rest of it, she saw now, was spitting fat and popping bits of gristle in the bonfire. The melting flesh revealed a too-familiar skeleton, and her stomach turned again. Not so long ago, people had rioted against anatomists because they believed you could not enter Heaven with your body in pieces. What, then, happened to a body that was decapitated and burned, an innocent thing ripped to shreds by the crowd? Did creatures of the Other Place go to the same heaven as those of this sphere?

"Bit much for ya?" The man leaned in, his arm still hot around her waist. All of his weight fell on her—he was too drunk to keep it himself. She shoved him, and he laughed, and she shoved him again as hard as she could and again he laughed and his spit landed on her cheek.

The hot terror inside her sharpened to a point. She wiped the saliva off her cheek with the back of her hand, and then she reached up and cupped his chin in her hand so he was forced to look at her. Sparks danced through her vision to match the ones spat from the fire.

"Tell me of the witch," she said.

His eyes grew distant, his face slack. "Not a pretty one. Flat as a board and dark-haired, and two goat's horns on her head. From her congress with the Devil, I heard. The beast ran to her like a lapdog, and that was how we knew she was its mistress, and when we tore the scarf from her head, there was the marks of her infernal nature."

Margaret. Another that the creature would have thought kin, and sought out for help.

Sarah swallowed. Over the roiling, shouting crowd, she heard Mrs. June yelling for her. She pressed harder on the man's jaw and this time he yelped softly.

"I want you to burn," she said, and for a moment, all the light went out of the world. When her vision cleared, she'd stumbled from the crate and the man's back was to her. His friends desperately held him back from stepping into the bonfire to smolder with that which they had killed. The last she saw of him before she fled back into the crowd was him pulling free and clambering into the blaze. His face blackened but he did not scream, not like his friends did.

As soon as it had come, that great power vanished from her. The buzzing in her head was nothing but the reverberating screams and shouts of the crowd; the feeling that she held all of destiny in her hand was just a fantasy again. But the rage didn't leave. It crashed through her in waves with no-where else to go now, rising as bitter acid in her throat and blood in her mouth where she'd bitten her tongue. The torches and bonfires choked her with their smoke and the crush of people spun on oblivious in their rioting festival, and oh, she wanted to snuff it all out, all of it. What good was a power like this? What good was a weapon like this, uncontrollable to her, indiscriminate?

She tried. She tried reaching for it again. She thought of Margaret in Newgate and imagined turning the will of the crowd onto the prison, using their bodies to tear it down stone by stone. But that sharpest moment was gone, and this was not Sir Christopher's tower with its miraculous geometry to forge her raw potential into a blade. Now she was just a woman sick with rage, deafened by the scream-ing and the ringing of her own pulse, and the crowd who should have feared her laughed and cheered all around at the chaos they did not understand, as the dark sky that harkened the end of the world fell upon all of them.

Sarah looked down at her useless hands. She could go and beat them against the prison walls until she bled. It would be something—a blood sacrifice, like the witches of old. Mrs. June had vanished. She didn't even know which way she was pointed now.

Then she felt it—like a string plunked inside her. That

invisible thread that connected her to the Wren child. Distress, pain. As London slid into wreck and ruin, so did the birth. Her own shuddering fear mixed with the baby's and stole her breath. It was a plea, from one uncanny cousin to another.

She could not get Margaret out of Newgate, not by her will alone. But maybe—with Wren, with the power of the Monument's position—

She had to get to the birth. Deliver the child. Use Wren's words and his Monument to finally take control of the power that rode her. Tear down Newgate, wall by wall.

Make the world as it ought to be.

When Sarah finally made it to the Wrens' home, smoke-streaked and panting, damp from tears she had tried to clean on her sleeve, the valet was waiting for her with an open door. He said nothing about her appearance but crossed himself as she passed. It was a night to turn anyone to omens. She did not need to be shown to Faith's birthing room; the screams led her straight there.

A maid rushed out of the room carrying an armful of bloodied rags. Too much blood this early, unless Faith had been laboring hours alone. She put on the offered apron, swept the thought of Margaret chained and imprisoned into a locked corner of her mind, and followed the screams into the room.

The laboring woman ran out of air for screaming and slid into desperate panting instead. Faith lay on the bed; the birthing chair was overturned at the side of the room and smeared with the fluids of gestation, red and clear and yellowish. She was on her back, legs spread and shaking from the exertion of merely keeping her knees up. Her shift was pulled up to her belly without even a sheet to protect her modesty, and at the sound of the door opening, she looked to Sarah with the wild, unseeing eyes of a dying animal with an arrow in its flank. Mrs. June knelt below her, sleeves soaked pink and red up to the middle of her forearms.

Wren himself stood in the dark corner farthest from the bed, in his undershirt and trousers, pulling from a clay pipe. The smoke and the smell of blood together made the air feel too thick to breathe. His eyes followed Sarah's entrance and then slid away, and that queer sickness in her stomach turned over on itself again.

Well. He was not important. Not right now. She dropped her bag and went to Mrs. June's side.

"What's happening?"

"I don't know." Mrs. June's tugged up her bloody sleeves. Whatever argument hung between them was meaningless now. "Her pains are off, the baby is low as it should be but will not come. I may have to cut her."

"All the blood . . ."

If the placenta had torn, Faith was dead already. But

Mrs. June shook her head. She put her hand on the inside of Faith's red-streaked thigh and pressed her leg outward. "Come, my dear, let's try another angle."

Sarah went to the head of the bed. Faith was pale as the moon, and her eyes locked on some bit of the embroidery on the bed canopy, the faraway and empty stare of an opium-eater. Sarah squeezed her hand, but got nothing in response. Wren, in the corner, shifted closer to the bed, with his arms crossed and the pipe leaving little ash-gray pockmarks on his white shirtsleeve where he kept tap-tap-tapping it in time with the mantel clock.

"Has her mother come?" she asked him. Strange, for a woman to give birth without a female relative or friend. And where were the maids?

"Perhaps word did not reach her in time to make the journey," Wren said. "The roads are bad, this time of year."

Faith's hand suddenly closed around Sarah's. Her mouth moved but what came out was too soft to hear over the clamor of Mrs. June shaking her bag empty to spread every tool she had onto the bedsheet. Sarah bent close, and in a burst of movement, Faith let go of her hand and grabbed a fistful of her hair instead. Sarah yelped and tried to jerk away, but Faith's grip was iron.

"Make him go," Faith said. A small trickle of blood and mucus formed on the edge of her lips.

"You said you wished—"

"*Make him go*," Faith said again, more air than words.

Sarah nodded, and Faith's hand dropped from her hair. A sharp pain still pulsed there that didn't go away when Sarah rubbed at the spot. She stood and turned to Sir Christopher.

"She wishes her privacy," she said.

Wren just looked at her.

"Wait outside and we will tell you as soon as it is through."

"She is my wife," he said, and she did not like the way it rang more of possession than concern, "and this is my house."

"You should leave."

Wren set his cooling pipe on the bedside table and looked at her with such genuine curiosity that Sarah felt like a stuffed bird under a glass cloche. "Will you make me?" He sounded . . . she would have said eager, but that would be lunacy. Sarah took a halting step back.

"Oh, for God's sake," Mrs. June said, hands slick with almond oil, feeling for the baby. Faith howled. "Get out. Like a man should. If you want your wife alive and your house with fewer stains, be useful and send the kitchen staff for more clean rags and water, and then stay away."

Wren hesitated a moment longer, but they were far too into it now for threats of withholding their pay or having them removed from the room. There came a point where their duty far exceeded their obligation to him, and he knew it.

"Sarah!" Mrs. June hefted Faith's leg over her shoulder,

tilted her pelvis so she was angled on her side. "Keep this clean so I can see—there, there's the head. Push now, my dear—push!"

When the long hours of waiting for the afterbirth were finally through, Mrs. June sat moodily in the corner drinking wine, her apron and hands and dress underneath smeared with blood. Faith had fallen back against the pillows and now lay in a murmuring almost-sleep, unable to be roused. Whether it was exhaustion or deeper damage, they couldn't tell yet. Sarah paced the room with the boy so he wouldn't cry.

Her head hurt. Pressure built between her ears like there was a thunderstorm coming. The fishermen hadn't prophesied rain today, and the morning skies were blue as anything, but she swore she could smell it. She tried not to look at the baby's face. Those prickly, strange hairs like fine needles. The extra eyes. Those ghastly bruise-colored veins bulging against his translucent skin. Perhaps with some sun he would turn a little darker like his mother; that would help.

It would not help.

Nothing would help this one pass unnoticed.

He opened his mouth and let out an indignant cry. The noise hurt her ears.

"Shh," she said. "Shh, little one." He had his first milk;

he could go a bit longer yet without another one. If his parents decided he should be allowed a second one. Faith did not stir, though her nonsense grew more fevered.

Someone tried the door. Mrs. June jumped. The wine in her cup splashed over her arm and mixed with the drying blood she had not managed to wipe off. The baby fell silent.

"Hide his face," Mrs. June said. No one could see him until his father decided what must be done. Two dead children in a row was a sorrow; a baby like this was a shame on the house. And the Wrens were very powerful people. Midwives could not afford to be careless with their patrons' reputations.

She got up and opened the door a crack, and whispered with the person there. Then she closed the door and tried again to wipe her hands on the soiled apron. "A maid. They want me in the kitchen to make sure they've prepared the caudle right. Stay here."

She left and Sarah turned the lock again as soon as the door shut. The baby squirmed against her. His fine hairs drew tiny pinpricks of blood where they sank into her skin. He was sharpness all through and through—sharp hairs, sharp fingernails, and when she'd put her thumb in his mouth to soothe him, she'd felt sharp teeth nested in his gums, waiting to emerge. How could a baby like this ever move through the world without cutting it to ribbons?

Someone knocked at the door again. Politely, insistently. Sarah froze.

"Mrs. Davis?" Sir Christopher's voice. She knew him well enough by now to hear the edge running beneath his politeness. "The kitchen girl tells me it is done. Is the baby well?"

She did not know what to say. The baby was alive. Was he well? For now. Wren had known he would be born strange, but who could be prepared for a baby they could not hold? Would he blame her for how it had come? She could not stand to see that faint pride in his eyes turn to anger. Would he demand she smother the baby, or do it himself? She did not know if she could stand that either—it was only an innocent, helpless thing.

He knocked again. "Mrs. Davis?" She thought the babe would cry, but he lay silent. He squirmed in her arms and one of his sharp nails slit a thin line across her chest. A drop of blood landed on his lip and he licked at it with a pink tongue, sated.

From the other side of the door, Wren sighed. A key scraped in the lock. Of course he had a key. He was master of this house.

The door opened. Wren was dressed, despite the late hour. He already had on his coat. Before Sarah could form a reasonable objection, he crossed the room and looked upon his son.

"So this is what I have made," he said. He touched the baby's nose delicately, and the child opened his many eyes, and for a second, father and son stared into each other. "Give him to me, please."

She shouldn't object. And yet the same kinship that had her knowing what this child would be before his birth tethered her to him now, and all of the many ends she could imagine twisted in her guts. She held the baby closer.

"Give him to me," Wren repeated, and held out his arms in a shape that implied he would take care.

"What will you do?"

"He is my son," Wren said. "I will do with him whatever I wish. And you will give him to me."

He took the baby. She thought about arguing, but there was no argument she could make that would convince him, and no fight that she could put up that would not destroy her. And that pressure in her head, that dark storm rolling in, clouded all her thoughts.

"Thank you," he said. "For your help." He looked down once more at the baby, and then wrapped it tighter in its swaddle and was gone.

Sarah sagged against the bench at the foot of Faith's bed. The floor beneath her feet spun, and the place where the baby had cut her burned. Poison? Or only exhaustion? Mrs. June should be returning any moment. She was probably haggling with the valet over their pay. She would tell Sarah the same as Wren had—it was his son, he could do with him as he wilt. And they would both be right.

The bed creaked. Sarah roused herself—there was another person to worry over, after all. Faith had woken but her eyes were glassy and bloodshot, and she seemed to be in another world entirely.

"Lady Faith, would you take a drink?" Sarah offered a cup of watered wine, but Faith didn't take to it. She tried a damp rag instead, wiping the drying sweat off Faith's brow, and this seemed to rouse her further. She reached for Sarah, but her grasp was too clumsy, and she grabbed at the front of Sarah's apron instead.

"My son," she said. "Where is he?"

Sarah forced a smile. "Being cared for."

Faith gripped the front of Sarah's apron with both hands and yanked her close with a strength that Sarah would not have thought her capable of now, not with the amount of blood that had soaked into the old sheets covering the mattress.

"Has my husband taken him?" Her hands trembled against Sarah's chest.

Sarah's silence was apparently answer enough. Faith shoved her aside and tumbled from the bed onto shaking legs. Sarah caught her before she fell, but Faith hissed at her.

"You need time to recover. Sir Christopher has the baby." She could not bring herself to say, *And so he is safe.*

Faith stared at her. Her eyes were as dark as Sarah had ever seen them, no trace of fevered confusion to be found. She burned with disdain. She reached up and took Sarah's chin in her hot hand, like a mother might hold the face of a misbehaving child to make them listen and understand. "You know nothing of what is afoot here."

"I am trying to help you."

"And my husband is trying to use my child for . . . for sorcery! And I know that you are a witch who aided him!" She stumbled away from Sarah, seeking a dressing gown, her shoes, something. But dark blood still trickled down her leg and she slipped in it and barely caught herself against the bedpost. She sobbed, but when Sarah tried to come close she turned away. "I will not let this happen," she whispered. "I don't care what he is, I won't bury another child. Or . . . lose one."

So she had seen his face, then. Sarah crept closer, and when Faith let her, rested a hand upon her back. The air had taken on a strange quality. It crackled around them. She feared that if she uncovered a candle she might set it alight. "You must tell me. Whatever's happening—you can't fix it yourself."

Faith stood silent for a long, long moment, gripping the bedpost. Finally, she looped her arm over Sarah's shoulder and let her take some of her weight. She closed her eyes. Sarah eased her back onto the bed, and Faith pulled the covers to her like they were another baby for her to hold. "My husband has always been an ambitious man," she began. "A brilliant man. Even when we were children. It's what I loved him for first, before anything else." Her sudden strength was failing; she lay back against the pillows. "When Gilbert died, he was distraught. We both were, but we . . . could not find a way to discuss it. That was when the strange children started being born in numbers. At first, he saw them as only a diverting problem in need of a solution."

Her voice went dry. Sarah offered the wine again and this time she drank.

"He told me he had discovered how the world was broken." Faith opened her eyes again. Some of the fire in them had gone out. "He said that this should be a world of order, and laws, whose cause and effect could be accurately and repeatably manipulated. But the influence of another celestial sphere made this world . . . unpredictable."

Sarah could see it. A man like that, told his whole life he was a genius, who so often had the laws of nature respond to his touch like violin strings responding to a bow. How might a man like that react when nature shook free of his control and came to claim his child? "He told you he could make sure the rest of your children were safe."

"We needed a bridge, he told me. Something—someone—of both worlds, who he could use to access that other sphere and work upon it so it influenced ours no more." Faith was slipping once more, overcome by her exertion. "You must understand. I thought he was overcome with grief. He told me we should . . . make our marriage bed, to speak, upon a certain place beneath his monument where the worlds are thin, and that would make our child into his bridge. I thought surely it was folly. Just something to give him a sense of control again. I did not know. And I thought once it was born—even if it had a cleft lip or some worse affliction—he could do nothing with his theories, not knowing how the other world worked."

But then Sarah had come along and taught him. How clearly she saw it now. His pride in her had been pride in his vision becoming reality. She had given him all the secret knowledge of her profession, and he would use it to destroy the source of their power. And worst—no, only worst to her, even though it made her stomach sour to think of it—the most she had ever been to him was a useful contingency.

If only she could stop her head pounding long enough to think.

Oh, no.

She knew now what that pressure was. The spark in the air.

"I will bring him back to you," she said.

Faith nodded beneath bleary eyes. "Both of them."

"I will do my best." She could not promise yet what she would do to Wren when she found him.

She nearly collided with Mrs. June when she burst from Faith's chambers.

"Sarah!" Mrs. June held a steaming pot of caudle and a

purse that was surely full of their payment. "Where is the baby—Lady Faith—"

"Lady Faith needs your nursing," Sarah said. "And I am going after the baby."

She ran from the house before there could be any more questions, shouting for a cab to take her to Fish Street Hill, and the unfinished monument that loomed there like a ceaseless watchman.

CHAPTER 10

When she had come to the Wrens' home only hours ago, the streets had been full of rioting, cavorting crowds all screaming their hatred of witches and the Devil, all drunk and laughing and vomiting in the gutter when they'd had too much of either, forgetting who their spouses were or what the law said, all glittering broken glass and ashes and gravel underfoot. Now the streets were frighteningly quiet. It should be near dawn, but the sky was the strange dark purple color of spilled wine, glowing like it was lit by lightning that never ended. And it was too warm for February. The air felt the same temperature as her insides, and she thought she might be unraveling, the boundaries between what was Sarah and what was The World becoming as permeable as the boundaries between this world and the Other Place. She had taken her bag with her, but she left it now on the stoop of a shuttered apothecary, and took only her knife.

She did not know what she intended.

Save the baby?

Save Margaret?

Save the earth and the Other Place?

She had no idea how to do any of those three. Something spooked the cab's horse near the start of Fish Street Hill; the driver could not get it to calm, and so from there she walked. The buildings leaned into each other, like whispering widows, their long spindly fingers gripping one another's hands and laughing at her folly as she continued on. The sky itself looked like laughter, great dark mouths opening in the clouds and closing silently again, over and over.

It occurred to her that she might be losing her mind.

If she was—was that not the better option?

The Monument itself loomed ahead. The strange light in the sky seemed to swirl around the gilt urn atop the fluted column. The little hairs on her arms all stood at attention. She tried the door, and it creaked open at her touch.

The darkness beyond was silent. She took up a candle, and descended.

She did not expect to find so ordinary a scene. Wren sat in a chair in front of the fire, smoking another well-stuffed pipe. His son lay still swaddled on a cleared table in front of him. The room was warm and quiet. They might have been any father, any son. At the sound of her footsteps, Wren breathed in deeply from the pipe and released three clean smoke rings, another one of his party tricks.

"Mrs. Davis," he said. "I hoped you would join us."

"So that I can take over for your son, if you fail with him?" His head jumped slightly, and she tried not to make her voice sound too bitter. "Lady Faith told me. How you . . . molded him into your tool for this."

"So you can see the world be remade more perfectly." He snuffed the pipe and set it beside him, then rose from the chair like a man far older than he was. "A world where nature obeys the rules that are set for it, where the cause and effect of disorder can be discovered and set right. Where you would not be able to accidentally murder your husband because of a power you did not ask for and could not control."

Her mouth went dry. She could not think of how to argue that, for Michael's death had freed her as surely as it had bound her, and that was not a thing that could ever be said aloud. "This may destroy him."

"Yes. It may. It is a small price to pay for a world no longer enslaved to a realm of devils and chaos. Does that look like a vision of a righteous world, to you?" Wren pointed up, and Sarah saw what she had missed so far. The ceiling was gone. Instead, an infinite darkness stretched on and on, lit only by strange stars in bizarre configurations. The sky of another world. She felt like she might fall into that vast, sucking void—her knees gave out and she found herself on the floor. Blood welled up beneath her torn stockings, and the pounding in her head spun up to a shriek. The baby opened its mouth, and from its gray insides poured a black, oily substance that drifted upward and joined it to the impossible sky. Its many eyes opened wide and rolled in on themselves.

You will kill him, she tried to say, but all the air had been sucked out of her lungs. The blood that trickled from her split-open shin dripped onto the floor, and, instead of puddling, began to draw a spiral pattern on the flagstones. And it would not have mattered—in grief for one son, the great man had decided that the sacrifice of another was an acceptable price to bend the world to his logic.

Wren staggered toward the table—the walls of the laboratory were disappearing now, replaced by furious, ever-changing images of strange creatures of fur and horn and swirling limbs dancing across a jagged landscape.

A strange noise broke through the din—the strangest noise, another voice.

"Did you think I would not—" Mrs. June thundered down the stairs. Sarah looked up, though she did not quite remember how to control all of her body, in time to see her stop short at the sight. "Oh," her mistress said, and her face went through shock and fury and disgust. "What have you shown him?"

Sarah had no answer. She had shown him every secret she had kept, because he had promised her they would do great things with it. Because he had offered a place, and because he told her he saw her for all of what she was. And here was the truth of it—he had seen her as a tool, no more or less useful than a hoe or an axe, and only worth his attention until the chore was done.

"Get up," Mrs. June snapped, even as a thin trickle of blood ran from the corner of her left eye. "The door is open, and I cannot walk through it."

"You wish me to break the world," Sarah said.

"I wish for you to make a world where you could have every ounce of power you have ever desired." Mrs. June grabbed a strap of her apron and yanked her up by it as if she were no more than a rag doll. "Though right now, I would settle for not being ripped to pieces because of a gentleman who thinks that because he has cataloged a thing he knows how to use it. If only I had enough of that Other Place in me to wield it myself, I'd throw you over and do it. But I do not. Now get on your feet."

She was right, for all that Sarah wanted to spit in her face. Two worlds hung by the slimmest of threads, and no matter what happened, she was the one person in this room capable of both acting and living through it.

Wren saw her coming. He was racked with great spasms from the forces that whirled around him but he snatched up a pointed compass from the table and thrust it at her. He fumbled for his book of equations. "Stay back. You two witches, I know you mean to stop me."

On the table, the baby's form had started to shift. One moment it was the shape of just a normal human boy, the next the face of a child from that other world made of shadows and edges, and after that it was once more the in-between child she had delivered. The black stuff pouring from its mouth had started to weep from its eyes and nose, too. If she looked too closely at him, she felt herself falling into a different reality.

"What would you have named him?" Sarah asked.

Wren's hands froze over his book.

"If you weren't condemning him," she repeated, though each word felt like another needle into the plates of her skull, "what would you have named him?"

"We had discussed Christopher." Wren did not look up from his book but a tear trembled in his eye and then was pulled into the maelstrom. "He may yet survive."

"He will not. He is too much of that place to live in your new world, even if he were old enough to survive being your bridge." Instead of moving toward Wren, she touched the baby's hand. Its fingers did not move at all. When she touched him, she saw how to take the power channeling through him. She could wrench it away if she was willing to kill him. What was one more baby in a world where so many died so often? Nothing, nothing at all. She could do it.

"Will you have your ordered world or your son?" she asked.

"You know exactly how cruel this world can be," he said, in a whisper.

"I do. Take your son. Let me do this."

He must know she did not intend to make his perfect

sphere governed only by the strict rules of logic. But she saw his conviction break. His hands shook, but he reached for his son and namesake, and when he took the baby up from that place of greatest power, the earth shuddered under them. The baby choked. The great swirling power, without a host, fell into chaos.

Sarah reached for that power. And with the door opened, with the walls as thin as they ever would be and the two spheres on a collision course, that Other Place reached back.

She had thought that it would hurt. And it did. Incredibly, ecstatically. But also instantaneously. It burned through her and burned her out, until she was not a person anymore but a boundary holding apart two worlds.

And God above, the power. She knew the world, in its whole glory and misery. She saw her mother back in Cookham fall to the pounded earthen floor of the cottage where she had grown up and pray that the darkness above was not the end of days. She saw a man in a land far to the east attempt the same thing she was, and for a second they met and recognized each other, but the geography his emperor's scholars had ascertained was not as precise as hers and he was destroyed in a flash of salt and fat and ash. She knew, too, the people of that other sphere as they also trembled before a strange new sky collapsing in on them and wept their own strange prayers.

Sir Christopher wept not over the world but over his son. The baby had not recovered, and here she could see why—he had far too much of the Other Place in him to have ever lived in this world for long. What Wren had wrought at his conception was an unprecedented fusion, not a bit of one world in a child of the other but a nearly equal mix of natures. From her vantage, she reached into the baby, prized apart the child of this earth and the child of the other, and returned each one to their correct domain. In Wren's arms, the baby wailed. For a moment, it had no face, and then it had one with only two eyes and a small pink mouth and soft fingers that would not cut. She left him a drop of his strange blood, because it pleased her to do so, and to think what mischief he might make with it despite his father.

She became the sky over London, and saw the last of the drunken mob huddled in terror as the stars disappeared and they looked up instead into the portal she had become and saw what so many of them thought to be Hell. She took some chill from the Other Place and used it to put out the fires.

The celestial mechanics pulling the spheres together shifted, and she gasped under the strain of keeping them apart. Inside her, the threads binding her to a form and a place snapped one by one by one. Inside the small room below the monument to the destruction of this city that had taken her in but never made her its own, three pale faces stared at the maelstrom she had become, but she could no longer remember their names.

She swept through the streets of London as a shrieking

wind. Men and women huddled in their homes, dogs and cats and rats in whatever corner they could find. The strange rules of the Other Place were as clear to her now as an English book—she could change anything she wanted, with a whisper. She could make this world one of complete order, no magic or surprise at all, as Sir Christopher had so desperately wanted. She could pull the Other Place closer, making everyone marked like her into a small god over the chaos, and for once see pride in Mrs. June's eyes. She could destroy them both and then lose herself completely, so she was scattered among the pebbles and dirt and storm-racked skies of the ruins. Every voice in two worlds rushed through her, begging, pleading, praying, hoping, wanting.

In Newgate, a woman sang in French, in a low voice that cut through the chattering, whimpering chaos. *Elle était une bergère,* a romp about a shepherdess. Sarah let it reel her in. She pulled the parts of herself back together, until she was herself enough again to understand the words and the voice. Newgate, that dark stone block, was nothing to her now. She pulled a rule from the Other Place and the bars became like clay; she pulled another and the lock chose to love her and open for her.

Margaret stopped singing. She could not possibly see Sarah—wherever Sarah's physical form was, it was far away from here, but she smiled. The crowd had torn her hat from her and stripped her down to trousers and a blouse, and bruises were beginning to show on her arms. Fury exploded in Sarah's chest and half the windows in the banks on Lombard Street shattered.

"You're here," Margaret said. "Or I've lost my mind?"

The manacles presented a challenge. Sarah was having trouble focusing. The delicate balance of the spheres trembled, and the Other Place brushed too close, and on a small farm in East Anglia a calf was born with three heads and speaking German, though no one would ever know, for it died as soon as Sarah braced herself to hold the line. She was forgetting again who she was, why this woman in front of her was so important.

"They're screaming out there that Hell has come to walk the earth," the woman said. "The end of days. Are you the end of the world, Sarah?"

The weight of the Other Place was crushing her. She could let it go, usher in a new world, a world where power would run through her fingers like water in a creek. The woman gasped, enough of the Other Place to feel the weight, too. She scrabbled at her chains.

Sarah wanted to let go. What reason was there to not set the world to ruin, when it had always left her alone, left her over and over again with people who did not love her and never would, who liked her small and quiet, and wanted her only because she was a tool they could use and discard? She was tired. Her grip slipped and in the churches the lead began to run from the walls again like it had during the Fire. Someone deeper in the prison started screaming as the iron in the doors turned to sand.

The woman's manacles dissolved. She pulled herself painfully to her feet. She was enough of the Other Place to live in the ruins after, Sarah knew. It would not kill her if she brought the sky down.

"I like this world," the woman said. She should run— these walls would crumble when Sarah let go. "*You* like this world, better than the alternative. You like birthing babies and you like the city and you like pubs and singing and reading the paper with some mum."

Margaret, that was her name.

"I know why you want to burn it," Margaret said. "So do I, sometimes. But most've them don't deserve what would come to them."

Margaret, who had touched her so lightly and said, *I think I know you.*

"This will kill you." Margaret opened her arms, though all she must see in front of her was a squall of dust and motes. "Make your choice, Sarah, I would not like to see you dead."

Margaret, who had showed her a life she might be welcome in, all of her.

Sarah felt herself losing again, losing coherence and the memory of Margaret's hand against hers. She held tight to it, that one single perfect moment. That was the world she wanted—the one where a moment like that was possible. She could not make the world perfect and just and free but she could set the world back on its axis, where such things were possibilities worth working toward.

She took in Margaret for one more moment that stretched out like sweet molasses, and then she looked for the Monument. She found the same point on that other sphere, and aligned them, and then began setting the other pieces of the worlds against each other so they were once again in balance. She found a soft point in the New World and set it against a lake in the Other Place that had no bottom, and in the city the ground stopped shaking. She found a particular sacred tree in Wales and aligned it against a rock where lightning always struck, and in America, a horde of six-legged bats flew back through the dark sky and disappeared. She found the power of a river in India and set it against its opposite, which flowed through the sky, and in a southern land yet unknown to England the beaches turned from red sand back to white. The storms evaporated; the sky turned the sweet pink of the promised dawn.

As the spheres came once more into their orbit, the power flowing through her started to fade. The door was closing, and she was stuck in the jamb. She reached toward the earth and London, and let go of the Other Place and all the power it could have offered her.

In the secret laboratory, Sir Christopher wept and Mrs. June raged, but there was nothing left in Sarah for either of them. With the last of her strength, she gathered up the bits of herself that had spilled across the world, and tried to remember what she had been.

CHAPTER 11

LONDON
May 1675
An end comes to all things

In London, spring brought tufts of green in the cracks between their cobbles and a return of the tittering goldcrests, the sick stink of the Thames and asparagus in the markets, ducklings in the river and screaming fights brought out-of-doors now that it was warm enough to yell. For Sarah, spring seemed to bring babies to Londoners as much as it did to the stray cats and nesting birds; business was swift.

This afternoon, her last appointment of the day was the Wrens' final check-in. Baby Christopher was nearing three months and due to be christened, and Faith was at the end of her lying-in period. They had reached the limits of Sarah's expertise. When she arrived at the house, a maid let her in and ushered her quickly past Sir Christopher's study. She smelled his pipe and heard papers rustling inside, but he did not emerge and she did not expect him to. He had not spoken to her since that broken night in February. No matter that she had saved his son—she was sure he would have dismissed her had Faith not insisted she continue. It was Faith, in fact, who had made her fragile new life possible, for once Mrs. June had cast her aside, Lady Faith had given her glowing references to several of her friends in the family way, from good enough stations that Sarah could keep herself afloat with only a few clients.

"Don't draw the curtains," Faith said, when Sarah was let into her bedroom. "I've a headache today; the light will make it worse."

She was very pale. Sarah sat on the edge of the bed and took her hand. "How is little Christopher?"

"The wet nurse says he eats greedily. Still small to my eye." Faith sighed and leaned back against her pillows. Sarah propped Faith's feet up and lifted her skirts to check her healing. It was coming along, though not as quickly as it should, and the way Faith's bones stood out starkly under her skin made her nervous. She had found, since that night in February, that she had earned an uncanny sense for the end of things. Something was growing in Faith, in her lungs and the mucus lining of her throat and her spine. She couldn't tell for certain if it was the effect of carrying a baby like Christopher, but she didn't think so. This was one of those terrible earthly maladies that Wren had begged her to sweep from the world. She squeezed Faith's hand again, and tried not to let the guilt weigh too heavy in her heart.

Faith, she thought, knew what was coming. "My husband has taken to him. I was worried, in the beginning, that he would not."

"How could he not?" Sarah asked. "You have a beautiful son."

"We shall see," Faith said. "He will be talented, I suspect, but talent can be applied to an ill cause as much as to a good one."

Nothing to be said to that—for all of Sarah's minor talents, she could not see the future. She said her last goodbyes; soon Faith would rise from the lying-in bed, return to society, mold her son as well as she could in the time she had. When Sarah left her bedchamber, it was for the last time. As friendly as they had become, Faith would not write or visit; their stations were too different.

She took the now familiar turn down the hall to see herself out, but paused in front of Sir Christopher's study. From inside came the soft scratch of a pen on parchment. She knocked, but got no response; she supposed her knock must sound quite different from a servant's. She felt no hesitation toward him.

"Lady Faith is well and can end her lying-in," she said. "I believe this marks the end of our acquaintance." The sound of the pen paused, and then resumed. She did not know what it was she had hoped for. No—that wasn't true. She had hoped for a kind word, some small sentiment to rekindle that warm joy when he had said to her,

You really are quite intelligent. How intoxicating it was to be recognized by a great man, and how cold to have that favor revoked. She dropped her hand. "Good luck in cataloging the rules of the world, Sir Christopher."

She departed the Wrens' with her purse heavy with pence and a heavier melancholy weighing in her stomach.

Her new rooms on the Strand smelled of coffee and chocolate—the heat seemed to bring it out of the floorboards, where it had seeped in from the steam from the coffeehouse below. She had learned to love it, the strange bitter scent mixed with spice and orange.

And what she loved more was fitting the key in the lock and finding Margaret inside, half-out of her sweat-and-alcohol-stained clothes after her own long work in the alehouse. She'd taken her hair out of its pins and it fell around her horns and eyes like a spill of ink, and oh, if there had ever been a holier sight than this, Sarah's heretic heart did not know it.

"There you are," Margaret said. "I thought he might have had you locked up for witchcraft, after all."

"Fortunately, his honor remains mostly intact," Sarah said, and felt that heaviness lift from her chest like Margaret had reached in with her strong hands and done it herself.

She locked the door behind her first, of course. And then she brushed the tips of her fingers over Margaret's naked back, the birthmark on her shoulder and the pink scar from childhood and the knobs on her spine, and Margaret smiled at her in the tin mirror.

The locked door would always be important. Two working women rooming together, and one a widow, did not draw as much attention from the moral reformers as two men might. But the respectability of a midwife was always so delicate. This room might be their one true world, where they could love each other and work their small magics and know each other wholly. Still—even if this small world was all they got, she would not have any other.

ACKNOWLEDGMENTS

The years of writing and editing *A Season of Monstrous Conceptions* have been ones of great change in my life, and though much of that change was wonderful and long-awaited, it certainly required the support of many dear friends without whom this book would never have been written. In particular, I could not have done this without the unwavering care and kindness of Cait, Jenna, Jesse, Colin, Calynn, Audrey, and all of my teammates on my queer kickball team (and as a sidenote—the fact that recreational sports have come to play such a large part in my adult life is the most delightful surprise). I hope I can repay them all in turn.

I relied on the work of several historians to make Sarah's world as accurate as possible, but I would especially like to mention Dr. Consolino and Dr. Teske for answering many questions big and small over the course of writing this book. As I was finishing *A Season of Monstrous Conceptions,* I also began graduate school for history and my cohort and classmates have contributed immeasurably to the editing process with their incisive questions and support. As I begin to think about the next stories I might write, I'm sure they will once again help me bring a bit of magic to the past.

I would also like to thank the many, many people who have contributed to this book on the publishing side, including my editor, Christie Yant, and agent, Hannah Bowman, both of whom shaped this story with their wise comments and insights. This gorgeous cover is the work of Andrew Davis and Christine Foltzer, and Jordan Hanley and Ashley Spruill from Tordotcom Publishing also deserve all the thanks for their work on marketing and publicity. I am sure there are many others whose names I don't know, but whose work has made this book what it is—thank you all.